CW00622028

The Adventu of Roderick Langham

Rafe McGregor

Roderick Langham is a retired soldier, disgraced police inspector, and reluctant occult detective. He inhabits the world of Sherlock Holmes, investigates cases with John Watson and Sebastian Moran, and is able to perceive the reality concealed by the illusion of everyday appearances. These nine stories follow Langham from his first encounter with the inexplicable in the Himalayan hills to his investigation of the wreck of the *Demeter* and his growing realisation that the dales, moors, and wolds which surround his Yorkshire refuge are home to an evil far older than the honeycomb of medieval monasteries and Roman ruins suggests.

Rafe McGregor is the author of *The Value of Literature*, *The Architect of Murder*, six collections of short fiction, and one hundred and fifty magazine articles, journal papers, and review essays. He lectures at the University of York and can be found online at @rafemcgregor.

The Adventures of Roderick Langham

Rafe McGregor

THEAKER'S
PAPERBACK
LIBRARY
BIRMINGHAM

Published April 2017 in
Theaker's Paperback Library.

ISBN (print): 978-1-910387-26-9
ISBN (epub): 978-1-910387-27-6

Website: www.theakersquarterly.blogspot.com
Email: theakersquarterlyfiction@gmail.com

With the exception of "The Wolf Month", which appears here for the first time, all of the stories in this collection have been published in or adapted by one or more of the following: *Theaker's Quarterly Fiction,* the *Sherlock Holmes Mystery Magazine, Nightland Quarterly,* Wordsworth Editions, One Voice Recordings, and the Old Court Radio Theatre Company.

Contents

1. The Last Testament

From the journal of Lieutenant Roderick Langham, Sirmoor Rifles (kept in shorthand)

I

December 5th, 1874.

I saw the thin plume of smoke above the hill when Captain Tomlinson halted our column at ten o'clock in the morning. We were enfolded in a sea of mist, which rippled wave-like on the slopes of the surrounding hills, leaving only the apexes exposed. My curiosity was aroused by a nearby crest, where I was able to discern a line of smoke rising into the sky behind what appeared to be a hilltop fort. My contemplation was interrupted by whispered word to report to the captain and I found him observing the native settlement with his field glasses.

"Ah, Langham, there you are," he said quietly – we had long ago learnt the value of silence in the jungle. "I want you to take your half-company up there and raze that village. I shall continue north. If you require assistance – which I doubt – send a runner. Otherwise you can catch up with us this evening. Any questions?"

"No, sir, but I don't think the village is Daphla. My scouts saw some of the warriors earlier. They looked like they were Lushai."

"Lushai here, near the Sub-Himalayas? Nonsense."

"*Havildar* Gurung saw them himself, sir. He's very reliable."

Tomlinson peered up at me with unconcealed distaste. "Perhaps you should rely on your own judgement and not that of your NCOs. You may disarm the village." He raised his field glasses again.

"Yes, sir, but the raiders were Daphlas." Our column of two hundred Goorkhas and coolies and a dozen elephants was part of a punitive expedition against the Daphlas. There had been no Lushai raids for nearly three years.

Tomlinson lowered his glasses, turned back to me, and wrinkled his nose. "Carry on, *Lieutenant*."

"Yes, sir."

I returned to my command and gave Gurung his orders. My forty-seven riflemen separated from the rest, melting into the mist in skirmish order. I took my position in the centre of the line, with Rai and Limbu on either side of me. Like the rest of the Goorkhas, they were barefoot beneath their puttees, finding the heavy boots I wore an inconvenience. The forest was dense with bamboo, creepers, and orchids, and we struggled upwards in silence, shrouded in white. We had completed about a third of the ascent, the mist thin and wispy, when I came across one of the strangest sights I have ever seen.

A crucified tiger.

The jungle had been cleared for a few feet around the pair of trees to which the beast had been fastened. Someone had slashed the poor tiger's guts wide open so that it was spread-eagled with what remained of its intestines hanging out. The smell was absolutely foul, a cloud of flies and other insects thick around the rotting flesh and fur. I passed the word for Gurung and he arrived presently, his usually impassive countenance betraying revulsion.

I knew it was a warning of sorts, but I was still struck by the violence of the thing. "What is it?"

"Nyarlathotep," he replied.

"What?" My Nepalese was coming along quite well, but I'd not heard the term before.

"*Crawling chaos* in English, *saheb*. I have only heard of the sign of the tiger until now. It is used by very evil men; we should kill them all."

"I was hoping we wouldn't have to kill anyone today."

Gurung retired and we pressed on, climbing higher and keeping our eyes peeled for signs of *panjis*, the sharpened bamboo sticks that all the native tribes employed as defences. Shortly after we had left the mist behind, Limbu grabbed my arm and crouched low. When I was safely on my haunches, he pointed above us. I made out a carefully-concealed block-house perched on the summit of a narrow ridge, thickly-set around with *panjis* and adorned with human skulls. I drew my revolver and passed the word for Gurung to reconnoitre. Ten minutes later, one of his *lance-naiks* reported it was empty. I ordered the advance. I could now see the walls of the village, the ridge which rose up above it, and the thin line of smoke above that.

Crack!

Another crack cut through the atmosphere and I heard the sound of dozens of boulders bouncing down the slope towards us through the bamboo.

"Look out!" I cried. "Look out, a stone shoot, a stone shoot!" I dived from the path of a boulder. Rai was too slow – the rock carried him off down the slope with a sickening crunch. I leapt to my feet to take charge as the trees around us erupted with gunshots. I put down some suppressing fire, bellowed orders for assault in sections, and made sure Limbu was with me. Then I scanned the trees for the centre of our line, broke cover, and knew no more.

II

I became aware of a terrible pain, but couldn't identify its origin or location. As my consciousness revived, I realised that my head was pounding and my throat red-raw and aching. I opened my eyes to find my vision blurred. I rubbed them, wiped the sweat from my face, and discovered a bandage on my head. I was lying on a mat in a room in a bamboo hut. I saw a water jug fashioned from bamboo next to me and gulped the contents down. My tunic was covered in blood, but when I touched the bandage, I could tell the wound was no longer bleeding. I didn't even know what had hit me. I started to rise, though all my muscles and sinews were afire, and heard footsteps from the next room. I thought it prudent to remain submissive until I was stronger so I merely raised myself to a seated position.

The man who entered the room was about five and a half feet tall, muscular, and clean-shaven. He wore a cane helmet with a bearskin crest, a reddish-brown takin-skin jacket, and small white loincloth. He had a *dao* at his waist, large brass earrings, and a tiger's tooth around his neck. His bearing was proud and intelligent. I was surprised at his dress and armament, drawn as they were from a number of different tribes. He folded his sinewy arms over his chest and looked at me: "English?"

"Yes, I am English. Lushai?"

He nodded. "Lushai to you, Mizo to me. My name is Vanhela and I am chief here. How is your injury?" His English was perfect, albeit spoken with a strong accent.

"Fine, thank you. My name is Langham. Why did you fire on us?"

He squatted down on his haunches so that our eyes were level. "Because you must stay away from here."

"Why are you here, in the Daphla lands, when your tribe lives to the south?" I asked.

"Because I have a sacred trust. This is a prison and I am its guardian."

I didn't understand, but before I could ask him another question I had a sudden thought that I was the only survivor of the engagement.

"Where are the Goorkhas? My soldiers."

"They have gone back down. Some were killed, but they took all the bodies with them – except for yours, for which we fought." I tried to push myself forward with my right hand and to grab Vanhela with my left. He rose and stepped back, out of reach, arms still folded. He waited for my strength to fail, which did not take long. "It was necessary. It was also necessary that I bring you here."

"Why?"

"So I can show you and let you go back to your chief, so you can tell him to keep away from Vanhela's village."

There was no chance of that now, even if they did let me go, but I did not think it prudent to share that information. I repeated, "Why?"

"Because of the Migo."

I knew that "migou" was the name for yetis, the mythical creature of the Himalayas, but they were supposed to live above the snowline, not in the jungle. "What is a migo?"

"The crawling chaos. Come, I will take you."

III

Vanhela and a warrior wearing a cotton sheet over his loincloth assisted me down the steps from the veranda of the hut. The warrior's cloak was dyed dark blue with a crimson stripe, which meant that he had either wealth or status, yet he deferred to Vanhela without hesitation. Once I was on the ground, Vanhela let go of me and I supported myself by holding the warrior's shoulder. I saw about ten huts in the stockade, situated so as to maximise privacy and built of thick matting made of split bamboos with thatched bamboo leaf roofs. There was no space for cultivation within the fort, nor were there any animals, not even goats. The air smelled of burning wood. We passed several warriors, all wearing the same as my helper and all armed with muskets. Some carried bamboo bows and quivers as well. The fort was walled on three sides and we were walking towards the fourth, which consisted of a sheer sandstone slope rising to the low ridge I had noticed from below. I reached for my watch: three o'clock in the afternoon. I wondered how long it would be before Tomlinson attacked.

Bamboo trees and creepers grew from the base of the slope and there was a gate in the sandstone, which led to a cave or tunnel and was guarded by another two warriors. The smell of burning was intense. The warriors greeted Vanhela. He turned to me: "Can you walk?"

"I think so." My head was still throbbing, but my legs were steady.

One of the warriors opened the gate and I followed Vanhela in, hearing the crackling of the blaze in the rock and feeling its heat. A few steps found us inside a modest cavern, where a ring of fire was burning, creating great billows of smoke that eventually found their way to what looked like a natural chimney a dozen or so feet above our heads.

"Do not fear, you are safe," said Vanhela.

I was not afraid, but I was uncomfortable from the heat and smoke.

"Look inside," he said, pointing to the ring of fire.

I choked on some soot and the effort of coughing ignited an explosion in my head. I staggered forward and Vanhela steadied me with a vice-like grip on my elbow.

"*Inside* the fire. Trapped. See."

All I could see was a combination of flame and shadow dancing. Then I felt a gentle breeze from behind and some of the smoke cleared for a few seconds. I gasped, stumbled backwards, and held onto Vanhela with a grip that almost matched his. Inside the circle, the red and orange flames flickered pink, and that pink took form. I cannot be completely certain, but the creature was about five feet in length, with an outer covering composed of pyramided rings which reminded me of both a crab and a fungus. There were two sets of appendages that looked vaguely similar to a crab's claws and horns on its back. There was also a tail of sorts, where the body tapered, but the thing had no head, only half a dozen pairs of antennae.

"One of the migo, the servants of Nyarlathotep who gave us our name. Once, there were many, but they fought with other gods and either died or retreated to the heavens. Only this one remains and he must be imprisoned else he will destroy everything."

The horns on the creature's back started to move rapidly and I realised they were wings – bat-like, membranous, and foul. It started to lift off the floor and I tried to move back. Vanhela held me fast.

"You are safe. The fire stops the migo from travelling and it is not strong enough to control the minds of men."

I didn't take my eyes off it. "What do you mean?"

"The migo are the crawling chaos of Nyarlathotep. They move through the minds of birds, beasts, and simple creatures. Once the migo enters the mind of a beast he controls that beast to his will and he can move from that one to the next, controlling each as he crawls through their minds. In such a manner can he wreak destruction upon men and the land. That is why we keep this one here, where the fire and smoke keep him free from all creatures. There are no animals in the village. Anything that strays in here is killed. Do you understand?"

"The... *thing*... isn't harmful to men?"

"It *is* harmful, but eventually enough warriors – your Goorkhas and English with their rifles – will drive it away. But it is never alone, because of the crawling chaos and the birds and the beasts."

"Why don't you just kill it here?"

Vanhela spoke softly. "If it can be killed, I do not know how."

My head was still ringing and I did not understand what was happening. I did understand that my men must be kept away by any means necessary. All men – all sane men who wanted to stay that way – must stay away from here.

I looked at Vanhela for the first time since I had seen his prisoner. "I understand. Take me to one of the tracks the boulders made and I will go to my chief. Take me now. I am weak and must hurry."

IV

I was stumbling through the jungle when Gurung found me, close on half-past four. I was exhausted from the effort, almost delirious, and he and Limbu practically carried me to Tomlinson. I found the captain peering through his field glasses again.

"Good God, Langham, have you been tortured?"

I let go of the Goorkhas. "No, sir, they treated me well. We must leave the village. We *must* let them be, sir." I shot Gurung a meaningful look, but he did not appear to register.

"Nonsense. Now that they no longer have a hostage, I can enfilade the whole village without discrimination. You'd better get along to the rear."

"No, sir, you can't attack them. *The crawling chaos.* Gurung, that – whatever you call it – I've seen it! I've seen the crawling chaos!"

"I'm going to ignore that, Langham. You've obviously had a nasty bump on the head. Take yourself off to one of the medical orderlies. *Havildar—*"

"No!" I grabbed hold of the little runt with both hands and shook him.

"There's nothing wrong with me. *You* – you've got to listen to me for once in your bloody miserable existence!"

"Unhand me! Gurung, this officer is under arrest. Place him under restraint and escort him to the rear. Now, man, now!"

Gurung hesitated for a second, shrugged by way of apology, and belted me on the head with the butt of his rifle.

V

It has just gone seven o'clock. I am being detained in the block-house decorated with skulls. I think I have heard the last of the firing. Once the Goorkhas have secured the village the Chukma Coolies and the mahouts will move in. The mahouts with their elephants.

2. The Colonel's Madness

A military mystery

I

I was sitting at my desk cleaning my Webley when I heard the assistant commissioner's whistle. I set the revolver down and unhooked the speaking tube. "Yes, sir."

"Are you acquainted with Colonel Warburton, Langham?"

"I served under an Everett Warburton on the North-East Frontier. He went on to win a VC in Zululand."

"The very same. Did you know him well?"

I noted the change of tense. "No, sir."

"Good, because he committed suicide this morning. The cause may have been his debt – it was an open secret at the Bagatelle Card Club. Are you free at the moment?"

"I can make myself so."

"Then take yourself off to Ivy House, Hanover Terrace, and see what you can do for the man. Report directly to me."

"Yes, sir."

The assistant commissioner had also served in India prior to joining the Metropolitan Police Force and liked to think of himself as the guardian of the

reputations of his old campaigners. I wiped the
revolver, reloaded, and replaced it in the rig under my
left shoulder. Then I retrieved my hat and stick and
told Sergeant Melville I would be out for the rest of the
afternoon. I trotted down the stairs, nodded to the
constable on duty, and emerged into Whitehall Place.
Hanover Terrace was on the western edge of Regent's
Park, opposite the boating lake, but Ivy House
sounded like one of the converted mews so I told the
driver to use the coach entrance.

As we hurried along the crowded streets under a
bright spring sky I reflected on what I knew of my
former chief. During my brief and undistinguished
service in the Lushai Hills he had been an acting
major in the 44th Bengal Native Infantry in command
of a field force consisting of elements of the 44th, the
Sirmoor Rifles, and frontier and military police. I had
met him on several occasions and he seemed a
pleasant and capable officer, although obviously not
destined for a staff position given that he was already
in his early forties. A few years after I joined the police
I heard that Warburton had left India for South Africa
with his parent regiment, the 13th Light Infantry, and
read that he had been in the thick of it in Zululand,
fighting at the battles of Hlobane, Kambula, and
Ulundi. He had been awarded the Victoria Cross for
his selfless actions at Hlobane, been appointed
lieutenant colonel, and then retired a couple of years
ago. There had been some small controversy over the
late award of his VC, three years after the action, but I
knew nothing of the debt the assistant commissioner
had mentioned and there was little point in
speculating prior to the acquisition of data.

The park came into view and we proceeded north,
passing the white stucco terrace of Sussex Place and
making for the narrow mews entrance to Hanover
Terrace. The location of Ivy House, on the right, was

marked by the presence of a constable, while the walls to the rear of Kent Terrace loomed on the left. I knew the man, whose name was Raugh, an elderly and efficient constable from D Division. He was standing outside the pedestrian entrance to Ivy House, which was squeezed between carriage doors on one side and a row of timber-latticed windows that reached almost to the street on the other. There were two sash windows on the upper floor, with a tiny balcony set into the brickwork directly above the front door. My first impression was of modesty, a small house with little or no embellishment on a narrow lane with insufficient space for a hansom to turn. I paid my driver and touched my hat in response to Raugh's salute.

"How are you, Raugh?"

"Very good, thank you, sir. The duty inspector told me to wait for the detective division, but I wasn't expecting a senior officer."

"I served with the colonel in India."

"I'm sorry to hear that, sir."

"Thank you, but I did not know him well. What can you tell me?"

He produced his pocketbook, licked a finger, and found the correct page. "I was on my beat in the park when I was approached by a Goorkha servant who is known to me as Colonel Warburton's valet. His name is Ghale. That was at twenty-one minutes past eleven. He said that he feared for the colonel's life. I blew my whistle and proceeded back here with Ghale, Constable Clarence arriving shortly after. Ghale led us upstairs to the colonel's study," he pointed up at the sash window on the right with his pencil, "which was locked. Clarence and me forced the door and found the colonel slumped over his desk with a revolver to hand. I sent Clarence back to the station to report and waited with Ghale. Clarence returned at a quarter past twelve to tell me that a detective was on his way. He offered to relieve me, but I don't like to leave the scene of an incident until I've been properly authorised." He paused.

I checked my watch. It was a little after one o'clock; the machinery of the law had indeed moved fast. "You made no mention of checking the colonel for signs of life."

"There was no need, sir. You'll see what I mean."

"Does anyone other than the valet reside here?"

"No, sir."

I pointed to the study window, the upper part of which had been lowered. "Was that open when you arrived?"

"Yes, sir. I didn't touch a thing."

"Thank you very much, Raugh."

He nodded and noted the time of my arrival in his pocketbook.

I opened the front door and entered the house.

II

No sooner had I stepped inside than a small, wiry, middle-aged Goorkha emerged from behind the stairs, dressed in a dark green tunic and trousers that must have been very similar to his old service uniform.

"*Namaste*. I am Chief Inspector Langham of the Metropolitan Police. I served with Colonel Warburton in the Sirmoor Rifles."

"*Namaskar*. I am Bhanbhakta Bahadur Ghale, *Warburton-ji*'s valet and before that his *havildar* in the Sylhet Light Infantry."

The entrance hall was cramped, with a sitting-room on the right, a door to what had been – and perhaps still was – the coach-house on the left, and a narrow passage leading to what looked like a kitchen behind the stairs. The impression of modesty I had garnered from the exterior of the residence altered to neglect as I considered the interior. "The constable told me that you found him in the park at twenty-past eleven – is that correct?"

Ghale nodded. "Yes, *saheb*."

"What happened before you found the constable?"

"*Warburton-ji* told me not to disturb him after I brought the second post. I was in the kitchen when I heard a gunshot. I ran up to the study and called out. There was no answer. I tried to open the door, but it was locked. I tried to force the door, but I am not strong enough. I ran to the park for a constable."

"What happened when you did open the door?"

"We found *Warburton-ji* inside. He was dead. The constables told me not to go in and not to leave the house. I have followed their orders."

"I want to save the colonel from any scandal, Ghale, so I must ask you this question: do you know if he was short of money?"

Ghale nodded again. "Yes, *saheb*. *Warburton-ji* has the madness of the cards."

"Do you know how much he lost?"

"Everything." He touched his tunic. "This is my old uniform. *Warburton-ji* had no money left, but he said he was going to make more."

"From the cards?"

"No, *saheb*, from his book. *Warburton-ji* fought in many campaigns: Crimea, Mutiny, Zululand, and also the North-East Frontier and Cape Frontier."

"When was it going to be published?"

"*Warburton-ji* said very soon."

"Thank you. Would you show me the study?"

"This way, *saheb*."

I followed the little man upstairs. There were four rooms on the upper floor: a master bedroom, second bedroom, study, and bathroom. The study door was closed. As I opened it, I noted the splintered frame adjacent to the lock. The room was furnished with a large writing desk that took up most of the space on the side closest to the street, with three large bookcases covering the other walls. A tiger-skin was spread over a well-worn black and amber carpet. Faded glossy curtains were drawn back from the sash window. Warburton – I assumed it was he – sat on his chair with his upper body slumped over the desk. His left cheek lay on his left arm, which extended across the desktop, fingers pointing at the door. He had been shot in the right temple and although I could not see the exit wound, the amount of blood that had spilled over the desk and congealed on the carpet suggested it was large. A Webley revolver – the British Bulldog not the Royal Irish Constabulary model I used – lay on the desk to Warburton's right, as if he had dropped it after firing. Aside from the usual writing and smoking paraphernalia, there was also a tin, a salver, an opened envelope, and a bloodstained piece of paper.

"What time did you last see the colonel alive?" I asked Ghale.

"I delivered the post at quarter to ten. A few minutes later *Warburton-ji* rang and asked not to be disturbed until further notice."

I noted the bell-pull in the corner. "What letters did the colonel receive?"

"Just one. I think that is it on his table."

"Thank you, Ghale. I'd appreciate it if you could remain in the house until I'm finished."

He nodded and departed.

I entered the room, closed the door behind me, and discarded my hat and stick. Then I hung my coat on the corner of the closest bookcase and rolled up my sleeves. I had not brought my evidence collection equipment with me, but I withdrew the magnifying glass I always carried from my coat pocket. The way in which Warburton was slumped over his desk was consistent with him having shot himself in the right temple with his Bulldog while being seated at his desk. The pattern of blood on the desk implied that he had been facing south, with the window to his right, when he shot himself. I examined the stains on the tiger-skin, which consisted of blood and small pieces of brain matter, bone, and flesh. The exit wound had spattered this material from west to east, across the desk, carpet, and skin. There were a few similar marks on the bookcase in front of the desk and their height indicated that Warburton had been standing rather than sitting when he had fired. He had then collapsed over his desk and slid back into his chair, with the blood from the exit wound flowing off the desk onto the carpet, where it pooled. I stepped around the blood and desk, approaching Warburton's body from the south. There was no blood on the carpet between the desk and the window or on the curtains. The entry wound was quite high on his temple, which was free from gunpowder. This was unusual, although inconclusive, as the Webley fired much cleaner than previous makes of revolver. I leaned over the desk and examined the muzzle, which was lightly dusted with gunpowder. I was in two minds as to whether to examine the weapon or the letter first, but opted for the latter as the potential efficient cause of the suicide. The envelope on the salver was addressed to Warburton. I used my penknife to extract the bloodstained letter from underneath Warburton's outstretched arm while three flies buzzed around my head. I wiped the letter, which consisted of two pages, with my handkerchief.

The first page was from Major G.E. Lytton-Whyte VC, dated the previous day, with the following content:

It has come to my attention that you have

secured a publisher for your account of the Zululand campaign. Your false accusations about Hlobane have already come close to tarnishing my reputation and I cannot allow you to proceed with publication. Should you do so, I shall send the letter you wrote to Colonel Hammond dated April 6th 1879 to the "Times" and the "Standard" so that everyone will know that you begged your VC. As proof of my possession thereof, I have enclosed a copy of the relevant extracts.

The second page was typed and consisted of two short paragraphs:

Our work is still cut out for us and many a fine soldier will be lost before the war is over. I enclose copies of my reports. They will I feel sure interest you, and the General will probably like to look over them. I have I believe been fortunate enough to be mentioned in the official despatches. They all say that I ought to get the VC for saving young Morrison's life at the risk of my own, but Colonel Winter being a VC man himself it is said (I do not know with what foundation) does not care to increase the number more than he can help.

It is also said that there is an objection to recommending Field Officers but that seems absurd. I do not at all know myself whether I deserve it, but if I do it seems very hard that I should not get it. The statement from young Morrison was sent to Colonel Winter. Do you think I deserve it? If so, can you assist me in the matter? You have connections with the Press, and in that way (of course without compromising me in any way) you might bring public opinion to bear. I think it likely that the "Specials" of the "Times" and "Standard" will report my case, and

*if so you could easily work it without
compromising me. Remember I only ask you to
do this if you think I thoroughly deserve it
otherwise I would not have it at any price.*

The case appeared depressingly inevitable.
Warburton's memoirs contained some information
about Lytton-White's conduct at the Battle of Hlobane
that the latter did not wish to see in print and he
threatened to expose Warburton's begging of the VC if
the book was published. This was bad enough for any
gentleman, but if Warburton was relying on book sales
to relieve his debt, then it was doubly damaging for no
one would buy the memoirs of a man who was known
to have begged his VC. I set both pages of the letter
down on the salver and looked out of the window. The
study was slightly higher than the wall at the rear of
Kent Terrace, but most of the residents of the latter
had planted trees to afford them privacy from the
mews. I could see the back of the house directly
opposite, rising three floors above the street. I raised
the inner panel of the window first and then the outer
one. I leaned outside, my head a few feet above
Raugh's helmet.

"Constable."

He turned and looked up at me. "Yes, sir?"

"I needn't detain you any longer. You may go."

III

There was at least one flaw in the suicide scenario. Not
the lack of gunpowder on Warburton's temple, but the
lack of the smell of gunpowder in the room. Granted,
Warburton had been sitting next to an open window
and I had arrived nearly two hours after the discharge
of the revolver, but I should still have been able to
smell the cordite. That is the second surprise battle

brings, after the noise, the stench of gunpowder and, later, the stench of death. I picked up the Bulldog and opened the cylinder. There was only one cartridge, whose primer had been depressed by the firing pin. I extracted it and sniffed both ends of the barrel. The weapon had not been cleaned since it had last been fired, but it had not been fired in the immediate past. Using my glass, I examined the weapon minutely, finding no traces of blood. Like the absence of gunpowder on Warburton, it was inconclusive but suggestive. I placed the cartridge in my pocket and the revolver on the salver. I picked up the tin on the desktop and opened it. I recognised the contents immediately: the two wire brushes, small chain, and miniature canister of oil were identical to the cleaning kit I had been using when the assistant commissioner whistled. I replaced the tin, rang the bell-pull, and walked back around the desk and tiger-skin. A few moments later, there was a knock at the door.

"Come in."

Ghale entered with a decanter and glass on a small silver tray. "I brought you a drink, *Langham-ji*." He had already poured a soldier-sized measure of whisky into a tumbler.

"Very good of you, Ghale, I'm obliged." I swigged the lot down in one grateful gulp and returned the tumbler to the tray.

"One more?"

"No, thank you." There was nowhere to place the tray so he continued to hold it. "Allow me." I took the tray from him and set it on the only empty and unbloodied corner of the desk.

"*Dhanybhad.*" He stood up straight with his hands clasped behind his back and feet shoulder-width apart, at ease.

"May I assume that the colonel was not married?"

"No, *saheb.*"

"Did he have any family?"

"*Warburton-ji* has a brother who lives in Shropshire. I gave the constable his address."

I nodded. "When the constables forced the door open, did you remain outside?"

He frowned for a moment. "No, *saheb*. I was already inside when they told me to stop. I was standing here."

"When you were in the room with the constables, what did you smell?"

He frowned again, for longer this time. "I smelled my sweat. I had been running."

"Anything else?"

He shook his head, paused, and then his face lit up. "No gunpowder!"

"No gunpowder."

"The bullet was not fired in this room? *Warburton-ji* did not murder himself?"

"I'm not sure yet. There are two points that require clarification. First, the sound of the shot. You said you were in the kitchen when you heard it. Is that correct?"

"Yes, *saheb*, but... it makes sense now."

"What does?"

"I had just taken out the ash and I was closing the kitchen door when I heard the noise. I was not sure if it had been fired inside or outside the house."

"Then why did you run upstairs?" I asked.

"I was afraid for *Warburton-ji*. I have served him for ten years and I have never seen as much sadness in his face as when he told me not to disturb him this morning. And I saw the Bulldog on the desk."

"So you thought what everyone else thought – and what I first thought." I looked back at the window, squatted down on the floor, and stared up at the house on Kent Terrace, the roof of which was only about twenty-five yards away. "The second point is the presence of the spent cartridge in the cylinder. Do you know if the colonel fired his revolver in the last few days?"

"Yes, *saheb*, on Sunday. Baccy – his cat – had been hurt. It looked like she had been run over by a carriage, her back broken. *Warburton-ji* put her in a blanket, took her out to the garden, and shot her. We buried her together."

Three days ago, sufficiently recent to explain the condition of the residue on the revolver. "In that case all we need is the bullet." I pivoted on my heels to face the bookcase. "Come and give me a hand. If the colonel was standing at his desk someone could have shot him from the attic of that house there. If I'm right, the bullet should be somewhere here – on the second or third shelf from the floor."

Ghale squatted next to me as I scanned the spines of the volumes and the wood at the back.

"Here!" He pointed to the spine of a book entitled *The Naval War of 1812*. Embedded in the blue cloth of the spine above the name "Roosevelt" was a misshapen piece of lead.

I fished it out with my pen-knife and held it in my hand. The projectile was small and probably incomplete. I put it in my pocket and sat down on the floor. "Pass me my stick, please." Ghale complied and I lay down, placing the ferrule on the hole in the book. I propped myself up against the bookcase and pointed the handle at the place where Warburton's head would have been had he been standing at his desk. I ran my eye along the stick: there was a clear line of fire from the spine of the book, through the top of the window that had been open on my arrival, and into the attic window of the house in Kent Terrace.

Colonel Warburton had been murdered.

IV

I returned to Scotland Yard shortly before six o'clock, asked Melville to let my wife know that I would be home late, and locked the office door behind me. I was in a foul mood. I dumped my parcel on my desk, removed a bottle of brandy from the cabinet, and took two long swigs from the neck. It did little to ease my frustration. No.15 Kent Terrace was owned by the Duke of Bedford, patron of the Zoological Gardens, and had been uninhabited since the departure of one of the Duke's more distant relatives last month. There was evidence of a break-in through one of the front windows, which had been secured with a popular but unreliable type of fastener. On entering the house, I found no further evidence of burglary and none whatsoever of assassination, although there was a clear line of sight from the rear attic window to Warburton's study. I had made extensive inquiries at both neighbouring mansions. No one had seen anything, but I nonetheless suspected that someone had entered the house at night – probably, but not definitely, last night – made themselves comfortable in the attic, and waited for an opportunity to present itself. The marksman had taken the shot and then left the house by the front door, opening it from the inside. I emptied the brandy bottle into a glass and opened my parcel. I had retrieved the following from Warburton's study: a revolver, a spent cartridge, a part of a bullet, a history of naval warfare, a sheaf of letters from Sampson Low, Marston, Searle & Rivington publishers, a manuscript of *Campaigning on Three Continents: Volume I (Africa)*, and Lytton-Whyte's letter. To this haul, Melville had added two copies of the *London Gazette*, the latest edition of *Who's Who*, and a short memo on the whereabouts of Lytton-Whyte. Once I had packed my pipe with the oldest, rankest Ship's in my possession, I was ready to proceed.

The most recent letter from Mr Low, dated Monday, stated that both reviewers – Captain E.V. Earnshaw and Dr J.H. Watson – had responded positively, that Warburton's proposal had been approved, and that a contract for exclusive rights to the memoirs would shortly be despatched. The letter mentioned an advance of two hundred and twenty-five pounds for all three volumes, which was a princely sum for a new author. I turned to the manuscript next. The Battle of Hlobane had been intended as nothing more than an old-fashioned cattle raid on a Zulu mountain stronghold. Colonel Winter's plan was that two mounted columns of around six hundred men each would assault the plateau at dawn, rounding up the two-thousand-odd cattle and dispersing the thousand-odd warriors guarding them. His column would attack from the upper, eastern end of the plateau and Colonel Roberts' from the lower, western end. The raid went well until daylight revealed disaster: Roberts had been unable to reach the plateau from the sheer slopes to the west and a Zulu *impi* of twenty-five thousand warriors had arrived *en route* to attack the British camp at Kambula. Winter had no choice but to escape down the aptly-named Devil's Pass, during which discipline failed despite assistance from both Colonel Bannerman and Major Warburton. Warburton described the action for which he received his VC with admirable humility and apparent honesty:

I began the descent accompanied by Lt. Hudson (Coldstream Guards), who was on horseback and Lt. Morrison (Frontier Light Horse), who was on foot, his horse having been shot. We had only gone down a very short distance when large numbers of Zulus appeared on the crest of the hill, and seeing us at once opened fire and pursued us with loud shouts. The side of the hill was extremely steep and very irregular, with large boulders in all directions, and when we had got down about half way we found we had taken the wrong direction and were over a precipice.

There was nothing for it but to turn back in the face of the pursuers and join the right direction again if possible. Fortunately we succeeded, but by this time the Zulus in large numbers were within a few yards of us, firing and throwing their assegais. Lt. Hudson finding his horse done up got off, and as he ran along occasionally turned to fire. I saw him in this way shoot three men within fifteen yards of him. At this time Lt. Morrison became completely exhausted and sat down, and it was apparent that if I left him he must be assegaid in another minute. I therefore made him get up and run along holding on to the pack saddle, but the ground was so rocky and he was so done up that he could not come on, and I therefore stopped and managed with great difficulty to get him up behind me, the pack saddle having no stirrups.

My horse at this time was almost exhausted, and the ground rougher and steeper than higher up, and the Zulus having assegaid poor Lt. Hudson were all but on us. At the same time we saw large numbers of the enemy coming up the valley under us from the right and running hard with the intention of cutting us off from Col. Bannerman's men who were coming down the end of the mountain over to our left, and for whom we were making.

This was shortly followed by what was no doubt regarded as the offending passage by Lytton-Whyte:

The ground now became better, less rough, and my horse making a final effort brought us to within a couple of hundred yards of Col. Bannerman's men. As we approached, I saw Lt. Lytton-Whyte (Frontier Light Horse), who was with Col. Bannerman, leave the comparative safety of his men and dash for a trooper

*who was engaged in hand-to-hand struggle with two
Zulus. Upon reaching the trooper, whose name I later
learned was Rowe, Lytton-Whyte tried to lift him onto
his horse. The trooper had been* assegaied *in the thigh,
however, and proved difficult to lift. When he noticed
that half a dozen more Zulus were closing on him,
Lytton-Whyte pushed Rowe away and fled, leaving him
to his death. When we reached Kambula, Lytton-Whyte
claimed that he had wrenched his back so badly that he
had been unable to dismount to assist Rowe. I saw no
evidence of injury to Lytton-Whyte before, during, or
after the event and had he not panicked Rowe's life
would almost certainly have been saved.*

Winter had recommended both Lytton-Whyte and
Bannerman for the VC, but not Warburton, who had
received a mere mention-in-despatches for completing
the same act that Lytton-Whyte had attempted.
Warburton made no mention of his begging the VC,
simply stating that there had been a decision to make
a retrospective award after the end of the war. I
checked the dates in the *Gazettes*: Bannerman and
Lytton-Whyte's awards had been made quickly, both
on June 17th 1879, but Warburton's had taken three
years – not until April 5th 1882, a year before he retired.
I wondered how much petitioning he had done during
this time. Lytton-Whyte was a scion of the Sackville-
West family, had remained in the Army, and was now a
major in the King's Royal Rifle Corps. The Sackville-
Wests were related to the Russells – the Duke of
Bedford's family – by marriage and I wondered if the
connection was significant. The KRRC were garrisoned
in Malta, but Lytton-Whyte was on leave, during
which time he was residing in one of Mayfair's finest
establishments, Brown's Hotel in Albemarle Street.
The hotel was less than ten minutes' walk away, the
time was half-seven, and I thought the effort would be
well-spent.

V

The outside of Brown's was not particularly grand, but no luxury had been spared inside. The owners had installed an electricity generator the previous year and were currently installing bathing facilities in each room, a novelty that would make the establishment unique in London. In the previous decade, the hotel had hosted Napoleon III before he had decided to spend his exile in Chislehurst. Napoleon's only son, the Prince Imperial, had been killed in the last few weeks of the Zululand Campaign, a final embarrassment for Lord Chelmsford following the slaughter at Isandlwana and the shambles on Hlobane. I returned the doorman's greeting, strode into a small but stately foyer, and presented my warrant card to the concierge, asking if Major Lytton-Whyte was available for a short interview. I was directed to an elegant parlour, where I waited a few minutes before a porter came for me.

I was taken to a suite of rooms on the first floor, where I found myself in a spacious sitting-room with a balcony overlooking Albemarle Street. Lytton-Whyte was in the final stages of dressing for dinner, his valet flitting about him with a clothes brush. He was a tall, slim man with a magnificent military moustache and an entirely bald pate. When I was announced, he thanked both the valet and the porter, approached me, and held out his hand.

"I'm Lytton-Whyte, Chief Inspector, how do you do?"

I shook his hand. "Good evening, Major."

"May I offer you a seat? I'm afraid I don't have much time – I'm due at my club shortly."

"No, thank you, I won't trouble you for long. I'm

merely here to inform you that Colonel Warburton was murdered this morning."

He started. "Murdered! How strange. Do you know who was responsible?"

"Not yet."

"Well, there was no love lost between us, I'm afraid – but you probably know that already if you've found me here."

"Yes. I read the letter you sent him."

"He was terribly jealous of my VC and made all sorts of accusations about my conduct on Hlobane."

"I've read those too."

"He made an awful lot of trouble, accusing me of cowardice, Winter of favouritism, and then begging the VC for himself and Earnshaw. Earnshaw was absolutely mortified and resigned his commission."

I recognised the name. "Captain E.V. Earnshaw?"

"Yes, he was on Hlobane with us and was mentioned-in-despatches along with Warburton. When Warburton intensified his petitioning, he included the case for Earnshaw, but Earnshaw wanted no part of it. He was afraid he would be humiliated in public and resigned as soon as the war was over."

"And you were intending to humiliate Warburton?" I asked.

"If necessary, yes. He very much bought it on himself, Chief Inspector." Lytton-White moved over to the sideboard, where a pair of white gloves lay next to a silver double hunter. "I suppose I must be a suspect so I'll spare you the embarrassment of asking and tell you that I was visiting Uncle Mortimer at Knole Park, in Kent, last night and only returned to London late this afternoon."

"Uncle Mortimer?" I asked.

"Baron Sackville to the likes of us commoners." He smiled, fitted the watch into his pockets, and picked up the gloves. "I can have my man provide you with details of our movements if you like."

"Thank you, but I don't think that will be necessary. One last question, if I may? How did you find out about Warburton's memoirs?"

"It was common knowledge in certain circles. Warburton and I shared a card companion, Colonel Moran, another Zululand veteran. He mentioned it to me when we played on Friday."

"But you didn't know whether Warburton had secured a publisher?"

"No, only that he intended to do so."

"Thank you, Major, I'll see myself out."

VI

Eleven hours later, I stepped onto the platform of Millbrook for Ampthill Station. Thursday had dawned cold and gloomy and I was hoping the rain would hold off for my walk to Marston Moretaine. I had returned to my office after my interview with Lytton-Whyte, opened another bottle of brandy, and sought out the addresses of the publisher's readers. Watson lived in Baker Street and Earnshaw at Moreteyne Manor, fifty-odd miles north of the Metropolis. I had tried Watson first, as the closer, but his landlady had informed me that he was away on business in Hampshire for an unknown length of time. As it was then too late to call on Earnshaw, I had returned to my office yet again and read the rest of Warburton's manuscript in the vain hope of finding a clue to his murder. I fell asleep at my desk in the early hours of the morning, woke with the change of shift, and rushed for a cab to St Pancras Station. I had spent most of the journey reading the papers and smoking my pipe to keep myself awake. The fresh air of the countryside was invigorating, the heavens refrained from opening, and I soon reached Marston Moretaine village, a small cluster of half-timbered cottages on the northern edge of Woburn Forest. The rows of pollarded elms on either side of the road came to an end at a crossroad, where I turned left. Shortly, I arrived at a public house called the Bell and shortly after that, at two lichen-covered pillars supporting weather-worn gryphons, the entrance to Moreteyn Manor.

I passed between the pillars, walking up a winding drive lined with oaks until a sudden turn brought me to a small stone bridge across a moat. The bridge gave access to a sward, on the other side of which a low, liver-coloured Jacobean house was set between two yew gardens. I could see two sides of the moat, both lined with yews, and wondered if there had been a castle with a drawbridge in medieval times. I crossed the bridge and the sward and used the knocker to hammer on the front door. Dogs barked from within. A minute later, it was opened by a well-built man of about thirty dressed in a grey tweed suit. He was clean-shaven, with his hair parted in the centre and pouches under his eyes.

"Yes?" he asked.

"Chief Inspector Langham, Metropolitan Police. I'm here to see Captain Earnshaw."

He frowned. "I'd like to see your warrant card."

I removed it from my coat and handed it to him. He scrutinised the document carefully before returning it. "Well, you don't look like any police inspector I've ever known, but I suppose I must take you at your word. I'm Earnshaw."

He had a point. I had neither changed clothes since the previous morning nor bathed since the night before that. "May I come in?"

Earnshaw wrinkled his nose. "I'd rather you didn't. You'd give mother something of a fright. I was on my way for my before-breakfast smoke. Mother doesn't like the smell so I take it outside when the weather permits."

He closed the door in my face, but opened it a few seconds later, a cloth cap on his head and three spaniels at his heels. He led the way to a wooden bench that faced the eastern side of the moat. He motioned me to sit at one end while he took the other, lighting a cigarette. He inhaled deeply before turning to me. "Well, what is it?"

"Colonel Warburton was murdered yesterday."

He raised his eyebrows and drew on his cigarette again. "Murdered?"

"Yes, why do you ask?"

"Because he was heavily in debt and was about to cause a lot of trouble with his memoirs."

"Why did you recommend publication of his manuscript to Low?"

"Because it was well-written and as far as I can tell completely accurate."

"You think Major Lytton-Whyte a coward?"

His face contorted. "That morning on the mountain was hell – what did you say your name was?"

"Langham."

"It was hell, Mr Langham. We were all cowards. When we realised the whole *impi* was on our heels we just ran for it. I managed to rescue one of my men, a trooper named Gregory, but I left others behind. My horse couldn't carry more than two and I made damned sure I was one of those two. I was cut off from Bannerman's group so I didn't see Warburton or Lytton-Whyte, but the general opinion back at Kambula was that Lytton-Whyte had seized an opportunity to perform an act of heroism in Bannerman's sight, panicked, and saved his own skin. He certainly didn't have any back trouble – or any injury at all, for that matter."

Earnshaw finished his cigarette, ground it under his shoe, and immediately lit another.

"I've met Lytton-Whyte. He didn't strike me as a coward."

Earnshaw shrugged and drew on his cigarette again.

"He also told me you hated Warburton."

Earnshaw placed his elbows on his thighs and continued smoking.

"Well?"

"Was that a question?"

"Did you hate Warburton?"

He snapped his head towards me. "No, I didn't hate him. And I was here all morning yesterday before you ask."

"Was Lytton-Whyte lying?"

"No, exaggerating." He leaned back, inhaling the second cigarette with such force that I could see the paper disintegrate. "When Warburton found out that Winter wasn't going to recommend him for the VC, he approached a retired colonel named Hammond. An ex-Guardsman with influential friends in Whitehall and Fleet Street. When Hammond consented, Warburton took it upon himself to mention my name and we were still in Zululand when I received a letter from Hammond saying that he would do his best to get me a VC. I was revolted and I resigned my commission as soon as decency permitted. The thought of begging for a VC when all those brave men died on those slopes – it's, it's nothing short of disgusting." His eyes began to water and he turned back to the moat, finishing the second cigarette and immediately lighting a third.

"Yet you still agreed to read Warburton's manuscript?"

"I bloody had to! It was the only way to be sure that he didn't do more damage. Thank God he had the good grace not to mention me at all." He shook his head slowly and then seemed to think of something. "So even if I had wanted to kill him, I no longer had any need once I'd read the manuscript." He smiled, but the smile cracked and he looked away again.

"Do you know if Warburton had any enemies?" I asked.

"No, I don't. I don't know anything about the man and I don't wish to. Is that all?"

I stood. "Yes, it is. Good-day to you."

VII

I retraced my route to Millbrook for Ampthill Station, my energy and spirits decreasing with each step. Now that the interview of Earnshaw had proved an anticlimax, I felt physically and mentally exhausted. The investigation had reached an impasse. There seemed little point in checking on Lytton-Whyte's movements. First, I thought he was a highly unlikely suspect. Second, even if he was involved, he would have hired someone else to take the shot. I could do no more than examine recent murder cases for evidence of a marksman and hope that one or more suspects had been identified. I was not optimistic about the likelihood of success. As I approached the station on foot for the first time, I realised what a curious little construction it was. The gabled building was half-timbered, which matched the houses in the village, but it was also decorated in an ornate Gothic style that seemed extravagant given the remoteness of the location. I had been the only passenger to leave the train when I had arrived and now that I was departing, I found the station-master once again on his own.

"That was quick, sir," he said, touching his cap, "back to the Smoke, is it?"

"Yes, when is the next train?"

"Twenty minutes exactly."

There was a pause during which I expected the man to return to his office, but he did not. He was probably starved of conversation in this out of the way place and I did not want to be rude so I decided to ask him about his fiefdom. "You have a lovely station-house, although I'm surprised to see such elaborate architecture in so quiet a location."

"Yes, sir, that was the Duke's doing. Not this one, but his grandfather, the seventh Duke."

"The Duke?" I asked.

"Of Bedford, sir. He insisted that all the stations on his land were built in the Gothic. Of course, we ain't on his land no more, but we were then."

I had completely forgotten that I was only a few miles from Woburn Abbey, the Duke's home. The connection reminded me of the house in Kent Terrace, which reminded me of Earnshaw's alibi, which was that he had been at home all morning. *All morning.* I had not said anything about the time of Warburton's murder and the news had not yet reached the papers. "Do you know Captain Earnshaw from Moreteyn Manor?"

"Of course, sir."

"When did you last see him?"

"Yesterday at three o'clock."

"Where had he come from?"

"St Pancras."

"How long had he been there?"

"Let me think..."

"How long, man!"

"Monday. He left here on Monday, that's it. What's this all about, sir?"

I turned and ran.

VIII

I was back at the bridge fifteen minutes later, rivulets of sweat pouring from my skin as I gasped for breath. I stopped, removed my hat, and paused for a few minutes amidst the sanctuary of the trees. The little evidence against Earnshaw was entirely circumstantial. There were dozens of reasons he might offer a false alibi without being guilty of the crime. More significantly, there was a complete absence of motive. Granted, Warburton had proved a great – even grievous – embarrassment to Earnshaw six years ago, but Earnshaw did not harbour a pathological hatred of the man else he would not have agreed to read his memoirs. There was, furthermore, nothing in those memoirs to cause offence. I had only my intuition and my intuition told me that Earnshaw knew more about Warburton's murder than he had divulged. As soon as I ceased panting, I replaced my hat and pushed on.

When I reached the other side of the bridge, I was surprised to see Earnshaw sitting on the bench staring at the moat, precisely where I had left him. His spaniels had tired of his company. I made no effort to conceal the sound of my steps, but he appeared not to hear my approach. His cigarette case was lying open on the bench next to him, empty, the smoked ends scattered around his feet. I stopped directly in front of him, but he still failed to register my presence.

"There's just one thing I can't fathom," I said, deciding there and then on the strategy for my interrogation.

Earnshaw looked up, startled by my presence.

"Why did you kill Warburton?"

His face was contorted with grief. "Because he was responsible for the death of my dear friend Hudson."

I cast my mind back to Warburton's account. He

had been descending the mountain with two lieutenants, Morrison and Hudson, and had received his VC for rescuing the former. "I don't understand." Earnshaw was silent. I considered his domestic circumstances and was suddenly struck by an idea. "Do you mean he chose Morrison, not Hudson?"

He nodded. "Would you be courteous enough to allow me a few minutes' privacy?"

"Of course."

Earnshaw rose, left his cap and cigarette case, and walked to the house.

IX

I was not entirely surprised when I heard the gunshot. The sound was muffled, as if the barrel had been covered or the noise had reached me through an open window. I checked my watch to make a note of the time. I would be reporting to the assistant commissioner less than twenty-four hours after he had despatched me to Ivy House. I would be presenting him not only with a murder where none was suspected, but with a closed case that did not require a trial. It would be yet another feather in my cap. As I retraced my steps to the station, I thought about Earnshaw's last words.

Lieutenant Hudson must have been a very dear friend indeed.

3. The Long Man

A reminiscence of Roderick Langham, late of the Indian Army and the Metropolitan Police Force

---

I

It took me thirty-six hours to track the Macedonian to a village inn, in Sussex.

My arrival late on a Friday night and my haggard countenance both lent plausibility to my masquerade as a City stockbroker seeking a tranquil weekend in the country. I was just in time to join the other guests for supper, and our landlord – a *Signore* Rossi – introduced me to all four of my fellow-lodgers, including Makedonski. I was seated next to Edford, a cadaverous professor of European History at Brasenose College, Oxford. Without prompting, he confided that his true passion was archaeology, the practice of which had brought him and his two students to the South Downs. Hughes was a Welshman who didn't look old enough to be at university, small, dark, and surly. Parker was tall, fair, and full of his own self-importance. Either Edford was gregarious by nature, or perhaps tired of the company of younger men, for he spoke without respite.

Only he and I repaired to the parlour for brandy and cigars, the others retiring upstairs. Rossi set a decanter of Armagnac on the side table and asked if there was anything else we required, or if we wanted the fire lit.

We both replied in the negative, but I asked, "Do you have any cats about the premises."

"*No, no, Signore*. Not in the inn."

"Thank you, a very good night to you."

"*Buonanotte*."

"What's the matter, Langham, do they give you hay fever?" asked Edford.

"No. I can't abide the creatures. Vermin."

As our host retreated, Edford leaned closer to me and said in a conspiratorial tone, "Did you know he's quite the red, our *Signore* Rossi?"

I was nonplussed, but didn't want to show it, so I merely said, "Oh?"

"Absolutely. He was one of Garibaldi's Redshirts in the Austro-Sardinian War."

"Really?"

"Yes. Rather curious, don't you think?"

I did, but feigned innocence. "Is it?"

"Well, there he was fighting for a new Italy all those years ago and now he's living abroad. It doesn't seem right for a nationalist to be an expatriate. It wouldn't surprise me if the fellow was an exile, on the run..."

It didn't take me long to realise that Edford was not only garrulous, but inquisitive to the extent of being rude. Naturally I was used to such interrogations, albeit with a far more sinister motive. I kept to the truth wherever possible and subtly turned the focus of the conversation back to his hobby of archaeology. I knew very little about the discipline – if indeed it could be called such – and was quite content in my ignorance, but Edford's impromptu lecture served a dual purpose: it facilitated my continued observation of the inn's entrance and kept him from asking questions I didn't want to answer.

By a quarter past eleven, there was still no sign of Makedonski. I was considering turning in, but I knew I was too tired to sleep and hadn't drunk nearly enough brandy to subdue my feverishness.

"I say, you don't fancy a walk up to the Wilmington Giant, do you? I suffer terribly from insomnia, so I always take some light exercise before going to bed. I stroll over every night to check on our dig and smoke a last pipe."

"The Wilmington Giant?" I asked.

"Yes, the chalk figure carved into Windover Hill. I'm excavating at its feet, so to speak. It's only a mile away."

I assented and we set out into a cool, crisp, June night, under a glimmering moon. I'd hoped the fresh air would sooth my frayed nerves, but its effect was quite the reverse. We took a winding course from the inn to Wilmington Street, and the undulating landscape was filled with shadows alien and ominous in shape. Edford waxed lyrical on the respective abilities of his two students, and his high-pitched voice exacerbated my agitation. I tried unsuccessfully to block out the sound.

"...I didn't mention that Parker is the eldest son of Sir Roger, Bart, of Melford Hall, did I? I try and avoid it, you see, because the fellow's rather too big for his boots as it is. He's a passable Classics student, hence his interest in the Roman remains we've unearthed. Hughes, on the other hand, is quite brilliant. He's one of my history students, but I suspect his real interest is my daughter, who is a bit of a hoyden, I'm afraid..."

My thoughts turned to my own family. I'd neglected them to the point where the distance between us seemed impossible to bridge. When my son, Albert, died of consumption, I hadn't shed a single tear. I don't know why, I just did not have it in me. Emma pleaded with me to take a rest from work. But there was always an excuse: the Fenians, the anti-czarists, the Jubilee Plot. Albert died four years ago and I hadn't taken a single leave of absence since. It had taken an order from the assistant commissioner, two days ago, and even then I'd followed it to the letter, ignoring the intent: *get out of London.*

I did: on the trail of the Macedonian.

As we entered Wilmington village, ruins loomed up ahead, behind a high stone wall.

"I say, do you know that it was very near here that the scientific study of archaeology began?" asked Edford.

I bit back a harsh reply and tried to sound interested. "No, I didn't."

"Cissbury Knot. It was General Pitt-Rivers' first major dig – that's Wilmington Priory over there. The foundations are eleventh century, but the ruins are fourteenth. We'll cut along in front, next to the coppice. Now, I was saying about General Pitt-Rivers; he started..."

We turned onto a narrow footpath between the priory and a small but dense wood. Moss and the tendrils of larger plants encroached on the path. The wall was covered with lichen and creeping ivy, their roots eating away at the stone, as if Nature was trying to reclaim the building and return the Earth to its primeval state. I glanced at the dank, fecund wood and shuddered involuntarily.

Edford crooked his stick under his arm and enumerated on his fingertips. "...One, stratigraphic excavation, meaning layer by layer; two, the significance of the small find and the plain artefact; three, the use of field notes, photography, and plan maps; four, the publication of results; and five, the cooperation of indigenous populations."

"It sounds exactly like detective work," I mused, darting another look at the eldritch trees.

"What was that, Langham?"

I realised my blunder – the first ever – too late. "I may as well tell you the truth. I'm a police detective, an inspector at Scotland Yard."

"It's *Signore* Rossi, isn't it? I knew it! He's a socialist! Or a communist – no, an anarchist – he's an anarchist, isn't he?"

Although I usually err on the side of discretion, I thought it prudent to assuage at least a little of Edford's curiosity. "I've no interest in Rossi; it's Makedonski I'm watching."

"The Russian? Is *he* an anarchist?"

"He's Macedonian, and no, he's not an anarchist. It's more of a routine observation."

He gave me an exaggerated wink, and pressed a finger to his lips. "You can't fool me, Inspector, but don't concern yourself. I'm as loyal a subject as any; you may rest assured that no one shall learn your secret from me."

It wasn't his politics, but his habitual chattering I feared. Despite my gaffe, I felt relieved when we passed the edge of the wood, out onto a sward. The feeling was short-lived, however, and I grew uneasy again as we approached a line of massive oaks. Edford pointed over the tops of the trees to a steep hill. In the moonlight I discerned the outline of a huge man in a sickly, sulphurous colour. I gasped. "Is that him?"

"The Long Man, guardian of the South Downs. He is two hundred and thirty-feet high, but he's faded away the last few millennia, so the local folk marked him out with bricks. Come along, I'll show you our dig."

Edford strode in between the last two oaks, but I walked around instead, joining him at the foot of the hill. The row of trees extended away to our left. Immediately in front of them a curious garden consisting of alternating rectangular holes and semicircular piles of loose earth had been dug. Very close to one of the oaks, a canvas sheet was secured to the ground with pegs.

"There you have it. Half a dozen separate excavations so far and every one of them has yielded human remains." He produced his pipe and a tobacco pouch. "But that one there," he gestured towards the cover, "is a rare find. A complete skeleton. We're taking our time with old Scipio in order to keep his mortal remains intact..."

Edford's voice faded into the background as I looked from the giant to the trees and then back to the giant. A feeling of dread, or perhaps a wave of exhaustion, overwhelmed me – I saw a flash of movement on the periphery of my vision and spun towards the nearest oak, raising my penang-lawyer and reaching inside my coat.

"I say, old fellow, are you alright?"

"Oh, yes, quite. I saw something move – in the tree – it startled me, that's all."

"Indeed. You do seem a little on edge. I'm not surprised with all those anarchists trying to kill Her Majesty. Now join me in a pipe and I'll tell you all about the Wilmington Giant..."

He proceeded to do exactly that, expounding his theory that the figure was originally a Wicker Man, used by the Druids to sacrifice captured Roman soldiers. It was a horrible thought, made worse by the fact that there was much evidence to support it. I couldn't help feeling sorry for the Romans, even if they were invaders. When we returned to the inn, I knew I would dream of screaming, burning men – if I slept at all.

II

Makedonski and I breakfasted alone on Saturday. As soon as he was finished, he excused himself and returned to his room. I spent the rest of the morning smoking and reading the papers in the parlour. Makedonski didn't come down, but four visitors were sent up.

The first was a very large Russian, with a horribly scarred face, whom I recognised as Nevskaja. He and Makedonski had served under Karastoilov in Kresna in seventy-eight. I was surprised to see him, because we had no record of his being in the country. He did not stay long. The second visitor was obviously a sailor from his dress, gait, and speech. A merchant captain from Glasgow, I deduced. He left after a lengthy interview. I waited twenty minutes and was about to rise when another two men arrived and asked for Makedonski. I picked my paper back up, watching and listening as inconspicuously as I was able.

The man who addressed Rossi was about my own height, but much leaner, with a prominent nose and chin. His companion was shorter, with an athletic frame and a slight limp. Rossi sent one of the boys up with the taller gentleman's card and I was given time to refine my observations. The shorter man was a former Army officer; the handkerchief in his sleeve, his bearing, and his moustache bespoke as much. I was unable to determine his current employment without making my interest obvious, so I returned to his companion.

A cold chill run down my spine: the man was scrutinising me – with a skill at least equal to my own. He knew I was watching him and he knew that I knew I was being watched. His fingers were long and delicate, the hands stained with chemicals. His

movements betrayed the controlled energy of a
sportsman, but he was obviously a man of some
intellect. His employment was also a mystery to me,
but I decided he counted music and fencing among
his interests. I wondered what he would make of my
puffy eyes and weary mien.

The Chemist and the Soldier left a quarter of an
hour later. I waited a further fifteen minutes and when
Makedonski had still not appeared, approached Rossi.

"*Buon pomeriggio, Signore* Langham. You have had a
restful morning, I trust?"

"Yes, thank you, I have. I'd like my buggy, please, I'm
driving out this afternoon."

"*Si, Signore.*" He shouted for the stable boy, and gave
the necessary orders.

"It was very quiet at breakfast. I thought you said
you were full last night?" I asked casually.

"*Si, si,* we are. We have only six rooms, *Signore.*
Signore* Makedonski has taken two, one for a sitting-
room. The other three rooms are taken by Professor
Edford and the two young gentlemen. They leave very
early in the morning and I prepare them the cold
luncheon. They are digging for the treasure in
Wilmington."

"Yes, we walked over last night."

"And *Signore* Makedonski, I see why he has taken
the two rooms. He has had four visitors already this
morning."

"Has he? I didn't notice."

My buggy arrived and I thanked Rossi, tipped the
boy, and set off for Newhaven. I'd decided that
Makedonski was in Sussex for business rather than
pleasure long before his meetings. The ship's captain
could, of course, have travelled from anywhere, but
the nearest ports were Newhaven and Shoreham.
Newhaven's harbour was the smaller of the two – and
the less likely – but I recalled seeing a barque docked

there yesterday evening, when I'd hired the buggy. The *Lilian Younger* was still in the same place when I arrived and I took a drive around the port before lunching at the Dolphin.

I was favoured with good fortune at the public house, for I found not only an ideal seat from which to observe the barque, but also a publican much given to gossip. For the price of my custom and a few compliments, I was told more than I wanted to know about life in Newhaven. Of interest, however, was the following: the Glaswegian sailor was Joseph Munro, captain of the *Lilian Younger*; the barque was due to set sail for Shanghai via Bremen and Le Havre tomorrow; and the crew were very reticent about their cargo, which hadn't arrived yet.

I supped mug after mug of ale, praying I would sleep peacefully later. Several sailors left and returned to the barque, but nothing out of the ordinary occurred until early evening, when a loafer shared some of his tobacco with the crewman on duty at the gangplank. I lifted my field-glass for a better look and noted that the man bore a faint resemblance to the Chemist. The deception would have fooled most, but I'd become something of an expert in the use of disguises myself during the Fenian bombings. The Chemist smoked and talked with the hand for about half an hour before sidling off in the direction of the high street. I added the likelihood that he had trained as an actor to my mental docket.

I started to feel drowsy from the alcohol. I considered following the Chemist, but decided against it and walked up Castle Hill, enjoying the sea breeze as I climbed past the new fort. I toured the summit and found a vantage point from where I could maintain my vigil. My persistence was rewarded when, shortly after eight, Nevskaja – the Russian – boarded. An hour and a quarter later, with the sun setting, I reclaimed my buggy and returned to Alfriston.

I arrived to find Rossi waiting up for me. His night porter had reported for duty drunk and Rossi had sent him home. He locked up behind me, told me he'd left a cold platter on the sideboard, and bade me goodnight. I was grateful for the supper, especially when I found it accompanied by another decanter of Armagnac. I took the food and drink up to my room and gave full rein to both my appetites. The last thing I remember was lying on the bed and looking at the clock.

It was an hour before midnight.

___

III

I woke with an unpleasant start and an inexplicable fear. Something was wrong. I rubbed the sleep from my eyes and was immediately reminded of the Lushai Hills. Why the memory should come at such a time, I had no idea. I looked at the clock and cursed: it was already after nine. I cursed Rossi for not sending the maid up with my hot water, cursed myself for drinking half the brandy and bolting my door, and then Rossi again when I found my boots still filthy. I performed a hasty and perfunctory toilet, during which the combination of my unsteady hand and the cold water caused me to slice open my chin.

I stormed downstairs to find Rossi with a police constable. "What the hell's going on?" I demanded.

"*Scusi, Signore* Langham, *buon*—"

"It's not *buon* anything. I've overslept, there was no hot water, and my boots haven't even been cleaned!"

"A million apologies, *Signore*, but your door was locked and the girl did not want to—"

"Excuse me, sir, would you be a guest at this inn?" said the constable.

"Of course I'm a bloody guest here," I snapped.

"Now then, milord, I'll ask you to mind—"

I whipped out my warrant card. "Chief Inspector Langham, Scotland Yard. State your business."

He squinted at the card, took a few seconds to absorb the information, stood to attention, and saluted. "My apologies, sir, I'm Constable Hampton, East Sussex Constabulary." I nodded and he continued. "One of Mr Rossi's lodgers were murdered last night, sir. Professor Edford. He were shot to death in Wilmington. Inspector Brown come down from Lewes. He sent me to—"

"Mr Rossi, my buggy – and quickly. Constable, pay attention. First, I want you to make sure that none of the other three guests leave the inn. Professor Edford has two of his students with him, Parker and Hughes," Rossi opened his mouth, but I cut him off, "There's also a foreign gentleman by the name of Makedonski. I'll be questioning all three of them when I get back. If any one of them does try to leave, you have my permission to take him into custody forthwith."

"Mr Rossi just told me that Parker's already left, sir."

"What?"

"*Si, si, Signore*. The boy from Wilmington came here first. I sent him for *Signore* Hampton and I went to get *Dottore* Roundtree myself. When I come back, *Signore* Parker had taken a carriage and gone."

"If you ask me, you gentlemen from the police force should be looking for Parker. He bolted as soon as we heard about the professor." Hughes had joined us.

"I do not require your advice, Mr Hughes, but I do require your evidence. Tell me what happened."

"He was cool as anything at first, but then the boy came back and spoke to him. I was on my way to the kitchen to try and find somebody to brew the coffee.

When I got back to the parlour, Parker was as white as a sheet. He mumbled something about leaving and dashed off to the stables."

"Where's the body?" I asked Hampton.

"Where they was doing their digging, sir, under the Long Man."

"You have your orders. I'll be back directly."

I left my buggy outside the priory and took the overgrown footpath. I had a sense of *déjà` vu* and, even in the clear light of day, felt a minatory force emanating from the sylvan demesne. I quickened my step, leaving the wood behind and crossing the sward. A uniformed policeman and three other men were standing at the foot of Windover Hill, a short distance from the last oak. As I came closer I saw Edford's body lying in the exact place where he and I had stood and smoked on Friday night. The Chemist, bent double, was scuttling round his corpse like an enormous insect. The image was repellent and I averted my gaze.

I was able to determine the identities of all three of the men in civilian dress before I reached them: Inspector Brown, Dr Roundtree, and the Soldier, whom I could now see was also a doctor. "Inspector Brown? I'm Chief Inspector Langham, from Scotland Yard."

"Good morning, sir. The Yard? That was quick."

"I've been in Alfriston since Friday evening, at the Star Inn."

"The Star! You knew—"

"I met him on Friday night. I've told your man Hampton to make sure the other lodgers await our return. Now perhaps you'll tell me who the gentleman examining the scene of the murder is and what you know about the crime thus far."

"Yes, sir. The energetic gentleman is Mr Sherlock Holmes. He and Dr Watson," he indicated the Soldier, "happened to be in Lewes, so I took the liberty of requesting their assistance. This is Dr Roundtree, from Alfriston."

I acknowledged the doctors and asked Brown, "Mr Sherlock Holmes of Baker Street?"

"Yes, sir. You've heard of him?"

"My colleague Inspector Gregson holds him in very high esteem."

"Mr Holmes asked me and the doctors to keep back while he made his search. He's already recovered the bullet from one of the trees." Brown unwrapped his pocket handkerchief, and showed me a flattened piece of lead.

"The projectile is complete," said Watson. "Quite remarkable when you consider it entered and exited the professor's skull before coming to rest in the tree trunk. My guess is point four-four-two calibre."

"Army Medical Department?" I asked him.

"Yes, I served with the Berkshires." He smiled.

I indicated his leg. "Maiwand?"

"I had that misfortune. You are also an old campaigner; British Army or Indian?"

"Indian, the Sirmoor Rifles. If your appraisal of the bullet is correct then the weapon was very likely a Webley Royal Irish Constabulary Model. It's the most popular of the point four-four-two cartridge loaders."

"Because it fires double-action," said Watson.

"Precisely."

"And I should think you are wearing the exact model on your person underneath your left arm, Chief Inspector Langham," said Sherlock Holmes.

I was taken aback. I am never without the Webley, but it usually passes undetected because of my height, breadth of shoulder, and tailored coat. What disturbed me even more was that Holmes had been too far away to hear me introduce myself. His face was flushed, his brows drawn, and now that we were at close quarters, I could see a steely glitter in his eyes. "You are most perceptive, sir."

He turned to the inspector. "Thank you, Brown, my researches here are complete. If you will be so good as to allow the doctors to examine the body?"

Brown, Watson, and Roundtree left us.

Holmes extended his hand. "I am Sherlock Holmes, consulting detective by profession. I believe your business in Alfriston concerns Mr Nikulica Makedonski."

My jaw dropped open as he took my hand in an iron grip. "I... I see Gregson did not over-estimate your skills."

"Gregson? He is the smartest of the Yarders, although I confess I have not met all of the official force."

"How do you know about Makedonski? And my own identity?"

"My brother is employed by the Home Office. He has alluded to a Chief Inspector Langham as the head of the Special Irish Branch upon several occasions, remarking that the man resembles his name."

"My name?"

"Langham is derived from long, meaning tall. You are certainly a long man. Of late, Section D has turned its attention to Continental anarchists and it can hardly be coincidence that I saw you in the parlour of the inn where Makedonski, the Macedonian nationalist, has taken lodgings."

"In that case, may I ask what you were doing visiting Makedonski and subsequently disguising yourself as a dockyard loafer in Newhaven?"

He chuckled. "A touch Langham, an undeniable touch! I suggest that after we hear what the doctors have to say, we compare notes. I have no doubt each will supplement the other. In the mean time I'll tell you one thing which may help you in the case – if you would care to hear it?"

I was disappointed that Holmes' energies had yielded only a single point. Nor had his knowledge of my identity and purpose seemed clever once explained. I wondered if Gregson hadn't embellished his tales of the criminal agent's prowess. "Certainly, Mr Holmes."

"The murderer is just under six feet high, blonde, wore badly worn boots of a size ten, and is an expert marksman. He was also no stranger to Edford, and arrived here some time after the professor."

I was once again astonished. "How could you possibly deduce all of that?"

"Excellent, Langham! You have answered your own question: the science of deduction. I have applied my methods to the scene of the crime, but they are equally effective when put to other uses. In reading your own book of life, for example."

"My book of life?"

"It is impossible to deceive one trained in observation and analysis. Thus I can say with confidence that you served with a Goorkha regiment in India, suffer from chronic sleeplessness, remonstrated with your landlord before leaving the Star, and have recently been engaged in the protection of the Queen."

"You do not need me to tell you that you are correct on all counts, Mr Holmes. As for your description of the murderer, Parker – the missing student – is five feet eleven inches in height, fair-haired, and wears a size ten boot. And I'm sure he's had plenty of opportunity to learn to shoot at Melford Hall."

"He is missing? Well, well, let us see if the doctors can throw any fresh light upon this matter."

Roundtree addressed me. "Dr Watson and I are both of the opinion that Professor Edford was killed

between ten and two o'clock of last night. Inspector
Brown has confirmed that that Edford was in the habit
of taking exercise before he retired for the night."

"He was," I said to Holmes. "He also suffered from
insomnia."

"Thank you, Doctor," said Brown before turning to
me. "Will you be taking over the investigation, sir?"

"No, Brown, the case is yours, but I should like to
satisfy myself that the assassination was not a political
one."

"Your assistance would be most welcome, sir."

"Very good. If you and Dr Roundtree make the
necessary arrangements here, perhaps Mr Holmes and
Dr Watson will accompany me back to the Star?"

As I rode back with Holmes and Watson, I spoke
plainly of my indiscretion on Friday night. It was
possible that either Edford's loquaciousness or his
curiosity had put Makedonski, or even Rossi, on their
guard. While Makedonski and Rossi were short and
dark, Nevskaja matched Holmes' description, and
could have done the Macedonian's work for him. In
return Holmes informed me that he had been engaged
by Lloyds to investigate an insurance fraud and
believed the *Lilian Younger* of Panama to be the *Sophy
Anderson* of Clydebank, reported lost with all hands
off the coast of the Outer Hebrides three years ago.

On our return to the inn, we found Hampton in
command, with Makedonski and Hughes awaiting us
impatiently. Holmes went up to examine Edford's
room and I questioned Rossi.

"After you came back last night, *Signore*, I lock both
doors. I leave the key to the back door on the peg, but
I give *Signore* Edford the front door key because he say
he want to go out for his walk before he goes to sleep. I
hear him open and close the door half an hour before
midnight, but I am asleep before he comes back. One
of the maids says she hears a gentleman leaving by the

back door at midnight. This morning, I find the back door is locked and the key is in place. The front door is also locked, but there is no key."

"Did you or any of the servants hear anyone return in the night?"

"*No, Signore.*"

I joined Holmes and Watson upstairs. Until we discovered evidence to the contrary, it appeared that Edford had gone out for his usual ramble at half-past eleven. Makedonski, Parker, or Hughes had left the inn half an hour later. Had they left to follow the professor, or for another reason altogether?

"I have found nothing of interest," said Holmes. "I should like to speak with Makedonski."

Makedonski was waiting in his sitting room. "So, you are not Langham the stockbroker, you are Langham the secret policeman. Am I right?"

"I'm Chief Inspector Langham of Scotland Yard. You have already met Mr Holmes and Dr Watson, so I'll proceed with our business. What, exactly are you doing in a country inn on the South Downs?"

Makedonski took a silver case from his inside pocket, removed a Turkish cigarette, and lit it with a match. He smiled as he exhaled. The acrid smell of the smoke reminded me of waking this morning. "I did not kill Professor Edford. I came back to my room after supper and I did not leave it until I went down to Rossi's excuse for breakfast this morning."

"You haven't answered my question."

He smiled again, full of contempt. "I am taking the country air for my health."

"No, you're not."

"I think you will find that Mr Makedonski is organising an armed expedition," said Holmes. "When I asked you where the *Lilian Younger* was bound yesterday, what did you tell me?"

Makedonski said nothing and Holmes repeated the

question. The Macedonian drew heavily on his cigarette. "You remember as well as I do."

"Yes, I do. Hong Kong via Bremen and Le Havre. And yet Captain Munro told his crew they are destined for Shanghai. You would do well to pay attention to detail. The barque is in fact bound for Macedonia, is it not?"

Makedonski shrugged. "Have I committed any crime in this matter?"

"I believe you are innocent of the fact that the *Lilian Younger* is the *Sophy Anderson*. Did you leave your room at all last night?"

"No, I did not."

"Did you hear anyone else leave?"

"No."

"I very much doubt you had anything to do with Professor Edford's death. It would be extremely foolish to murder a hapless archaeologist while plotting another uprising, would it not?"

Makedonski said nothing.

"What are you doing in Alfriston?" I asked again.

"I am financing a trading expedition, Inspector. I was not aware of any subterfuge regarding the *Lilian Younger*. If you allow me to do so, my associate Mr Nevskaja – whom you will also have recognised yesterday – and I will sail from your shores tomorrow afternoon." He tossed his cigarette end onto the floor. "Never to return, I hope."

"You will have to use another barque to transport your arms and ammunition," I said.

"Quite so," said Holmes. "The *Lilian Younger* was impounded this morning and Captain Munro placed under arrest."

The Macedonian swore between his teeth.

I asked Makedonski about the previous night, but his answers remained unchanged. I made a note of his London address, which I already knew, and informed him he was free to leave. Holmes and Watson left for Newhaven, a few minutes before Brown's arrival. We commenced our interrogation of Hughes, *Signore* and *Signora* Rossi, and their staff – including the now sober night porter.

It was a dull and disappointing process, which yielded nothing new. Makedonski left before we'd finished and Hughes directly after. Brown returned to Wilmington to take charge of the local inquiries. I found myself alone in the parlour.

I tried unsuccessfully to relax. Despite my first good night's sleep in weeks – no, months – my nerves were still in shreds. I was about to call for a brandy, but decided on a pot of coffee instead. It was probably yesterday's over-indulgence that left me feeling so wretched. Before I could summon him, Rossi appeared with a scruffy youth of about eleven.

"*Mi scusi, Signore, Signore* Hampton has sent this boy to you."

"Thank you, Mr Rossi. What's your name, lad?"

"Sid, sir."

"Sit down, Sid. You've done a very responsible job today, well done."

"Thank you, sir."

"Where did you come from this morning?"

"The Priory House in Wilmington, sir. That's where I lives and works, isn't it?"

"You must have been up early this morning?"

"Yessir, I were."

"And the master of the house sent you to fetch Constable Hampton and Doctor Roundtree?"

He nodded vigorously. "Yessir – I mean nossir – it were the lady."

"You came here first?"

"Yessir. I weren't too sure where to find Mr Hampton and I knows Mr Rossi is always up bright and early. Also, I had the telegram for Mr Parker."

"You had a message for Mr Parker?" I asked.

"Yessir, I did. It was Mrs Wright as gave it me. Only I forgot. But then I remembered and after I found the doctor, I brought it back. I couldn't find Mr Rossi, but there was a gent in here. When I asked him if he knew where Mr Parker of Melford Hall was, he said it were him, so I gave him the telegram. Did I do right, sir?"

"Quite right. Did you see what was in the telegram?"

"Nossir."

"Did the gentleman say anything to you?"

He shook his head. "Nossir. He just said thank you and I hopped it back to the Priory."

I tossed him a shilling. "That's for your trouble, Sid, now off you go."

He caught the coin, touched his cap, and disappeared.

Had Parker's flight been nothing to do with Edford? I wanted to think without interruption so I asked the maid to bring the coffee up to my room. I considered Holmes' description of the murderer. Parker and Nevskaja were both possibilities, but Holmes had said that Edford knew his killer. That left only Parker. Either Parker or someone else, perhaps someone from Wilmington or even Oxford. Parker's sudden departure may have been because of the telegram. Similarly, the fact that someone had left the inn last night may also have had nothing to with Edford. Many a policeman has drawn an erroneous conclusion from mere coincidence.

And yet...

IV

"Chief Inspector, are you in there!"

"Hold on, man!" I lay slumped in my chair while someone hammered at the door. "Who is it?"

"Brown, sir. Mr Holmes would like to see us at Wilmington."

It was half-past seven. I glanced at the mirror and was shocked by what I saw. My eyes had large, dark circles under them, my chin was caked in dried blood, and scores of yellow bristles had survived the cold blade. I was pale and drawn, in dire need of more rest.

I would take a holiday – but only after I'd solved Edford's murder.

"There you are, sir. Mr Holmes asked us to meet him at Windover Hill. I was going to suggest a walk, but you look all done in. We can take the trap—"

"No, let's walk."

As we were leaving the inn, Rossi attracted my attention with a polite cough. "*Mi scusi, Signore. Signore* Brown say that my front door key was found with the professor. I was hoping if I may have it back soon?"

"Brown?"

"I don't see any problem with that, sir, unless you've any objection?"

"No, of course not."

"*Gratzi infinite, Signore.* And once again, my apologies for this morning; the maid—"

"Don't worry about it," I interrupted.

"And your boots, *Signore*, I sent the stable boy up to clean them at eleven o'clock last night. He says he did, but I have docked his pay."

We left and I pressed Brown for news. Sir Roger Parker of Melford Hall had died yesterday. A courier was sent to Wilmington in error, arriving late last night, and this was the news the boy had delivered this morning. It didn't eliminate Parker as a suspect, but it certainly explained his actions. We lapsed into silence as we walked up Wilmington Street and I considered Holmes' description of the murderer again. Five foot ten or eleven inches tall with fair hair and an experienced shootist. He might have used a Webley revolver, wore much-used boots of a size ten...

Boots.

What had Rossi said about the stable boy?

The weather had taken a turn for the worse and the Long Man's peculiar square head was shrouded in mist. Holmes and Watson stood next to the end oak, motionless, like two prehistoric sentinels. I remembered rubbing the sleep from my eyes this morning, and I knew why I'd thought of Assam. My mind raced and my heart pounded. Was Holmes always right? Not this time. This time he was wrong. I knew it.

The murderer was over six feet, not under.

"Good evening, gentlemen," he said. "Before we discuss the results of my investigation, I'd like to have a look at your revolver, Langham. You wouldn't object if I dry-fired it, would you? I should like to test Watson's assertion of the superiority of the double-action mechanism."

I hesitated for a second, then withdrew the Webley, and offered it to him butt-first.

"Thank you." He broke open the breech, examined the cylinder, and ejected the five rounds. He handed them to Watson and sniffed the Webley. "This revolver has been cleaned recently. Very recently."

"You were wrong, Holmes," I said.

"In which respect?" He closed the revolver.

"The murderer is over six feet tall, your own height actually."

"You are quite correct. I deduced from the length of the man's stride that he was less than six feet in height. In nine cases out of ten, I should have been correct, but I did not take into account that the gentleman in question is in very poor health and that his weakness reproduced the signs of a shorter man."

I looked into his sharp, piercing eyes, exactly level with my own.

"Dr Watson is of the opinion that you were not aware of your actions. I may have fallen into error over the height of the murderer, but you could not have deceived me had you known. Therefore, you did not know and I can confirm the good doctor's diagnosis. Nonetheless, I took the precaution of disarming you."

"Mr Holmes, this is outrageous! Chief Inspector Langham is a—"

"No, Brown, Holmes is right. I don't remember anything, but it must have been me. It could only have been me."

"When did you reach that conclusion?" asked Holmes.

"As I walked over. My final memory of last night is an hour before midnight. This morning I woke late, and when I rubbed my eyes I was reminded of skirmishing in the Lushai Hills. Because my right hand smelled of gunpowder. After I – *found* – Edford, I must have returned to my room, bolted the door, and cleaned my revolver..."

"But not your hands," said Holmes.

"No."

Brown protested, "But, sir! Doctor, surely this—"

"I have heard of similar cases," said Watson. "The alienists call it dementia. I'm afraid I noted the symptoms in the chief inspector as soon as we met."

"I returned from Assam with my vision slightly impaired, an ague, and a hatred of cats. I was convinced there was something else too, but I had no idea..."

"I'm sorry Brown, Mr Holmes is right," said Watson.

Brown sighed and said, "Are you sure, sir?"

"Yes." I looked up at the Long Man, his head in the clouds.

"And you'd better put the derbies on, just in case."

4. The Tired Captain

An armchair adventure

I

I remember the date very well. It was the afternoon of Wednesday the 9th August, 1893, when I received my first visitor in Baytown, where I had languished under house arrest for a little over five years. I'd been removed to the village of Robin Hood's Bay following an unsuccessful internment in a lunatic asylum in the seaside resort of Scarborough. My doctor had mercifully tired of seeing me in a straightjacket, and the relocation from under the shadow of the headland had improved both my mental and physical wellbeing dramatically. Indeed, I had not felt better since I left for the Northeast Frontier as a young man of eighteen, more than twenty years ago.

Despite my newfound health, I was bored beyond measure, and spent the majority of my time engaged in one of two pursuits. The first was writing a series of implausible adventure stories all too loosely based upon my experiences in the Metropolitan Police; the second was baiting the two disreputable detectives who'd been assigned as my jailers. Caine was an elderly ferret of a Yorkshireman, suspected of corruption to fund his gambling; McGinty was a gross, alcoholic young Munsterman. It was the former who disturbed my reverie on the day in question.

I had not slept well since the weekend and I was

sitting in a deck chair on the little promenade next to Bay Bow, my prison. The sea was calm and the day clear, after the great storm earlier in the week. I was enjoying both my abstraction and the warmth of the sun when I saw the Yorkshireman approach. He stopped a few feet away from me; out of the corner of my eye I observed he was agitated, turning a calling card over and over in between the fingers of his right hand. I did not acknowledge his presence, but chose instead to play the game between captive and captor which we had come to learn so well.

Caine broke the silence first; he always did. "Mr Langham, there's a Russian gentleman to see you." I looked up at him. "I said there's a Russian gentleman to see you."

"Yes, I believe you did." I returned to my contemplation of the sea.

"But you're not allowed visitors – not unless they've been approved by the assistant commissioner – or it's the police surgeon."

"Then send him away."

Caine had four years left as my warder before his official retirement and he was experienced enough to appreciate his good fortune in being allocated so comfortable a berth at the end of so inglorious a career. Though he would disappear to the races at York or Doncaster for days at a time, he was wary of making a decision that might jeopardise his pension. "His card says he's private secretary to Count Brusilov, the Russian ambassador and I don't want the count complaining to the commissioner, do I? See." He offered me the evidence to examine.

The prospect of spending the rest of the day on the second draft of *A Clue from the Deep* wasn't very appealing, but I had a role to play, so I let Caine squirm for a few seconds before accepting the card. It was made from the finest quality paper and embossed with gold lettering: *Captain Vladimir I. Gagarin, Private Secretary to The Right Honourable Count Brusilov.* Neither were known to me, but the arrival of such an eminent individual could only be related to the strange circumstances in which a Russian schooner had entered Whitby harbour, some six miles to the north, on Monday night.

I handed back the card. "I shall see Captain Gagarin if you wish, but the decision is entirely your responsibility as are any consequences that follow." I turned away again, marvelling at the tranquillity of the ocean so soon after the raging tempest.

Caine hurried along to the cottage, muttering to himself.

A few minutes later, I espied McGinty lurching towards me, most likely summoned from the Nag's Head. I smelled him even before he opened his mouth to speak. "Come along, Mr Langham, there's a foreign gent to see you."

Though I was delighted at the change of routine, I affected a sigh as I rose from the chair. I followed McGinty to the sitting room of Bay Bow and was highly amused when he stood to attention, swayed a little, and announced me.

"Mr Langham as requested, Sergeant."

Caine was rubbing his hands together anxiously. "Thank you, McGinty. Captain Gagarin, this is Mr Langham. Take as long as you need."

Gagarin nodded once and the detectives left us. He was a tall, dark young man with a stiff bearing, handlebar moustache, and a long scar running down his right cheek. I deduced that he had served in the army rather than the navy and attended a German university, possibly Heidelberg.

"Good day, Captain. Please make yourself comfortable and tell me how I may be of assistance to His Excellency in the matter of the *Demeter.*"

Gagarin's black eyes flickered and his mouth opened slightly. "I... I prefer to stand." His English was excellent except for a slight Bavarian inflection.

"As you wish." I sat in the wing chair closest to the fireplace, and produced my clay pipe and pouch. "May I offer you some tobacco?"

He shook his head. "If you already know my business, then I have certainly found a most excellent agent. You will permit me to ask you some questions before I state my purpose?"

"Please proceed."

As I prepared my pipe, Gagarin straightened even further, throwing his hands behind his back. He was nervous and I suspected his errand was as sensitive as it was urgent. "Thank you, sir. Do I have the honour of addressing Mr Roderick Langham, the former Chief Investigator of Scotland Yard who solved every case in which he was involved?"

"My rank was chief inspector and I had two failures early in my career, but I am the man you seek."

"I believe you were dismissed in secret. May I ask the terms of your... situation?"

I paused to light the pipe and savoured the blast of tar at the back of my throat from the Ship's. "I must point out that I was never dismissed and continue to draw my police salary, although my authority and duties have been revoked. In answer to your question: in theory, I may not leave Bay Bow except escorted by one of my warders and may not leave Baytown unless accompanied by both. In practice, I am left to my own devices so long as I do not stay out overnight. The police surgeon is supposed to examine me every six months, but I have not seen him for over two years. I find myself none the worse for his neglect."

"Your... health... has improved, sir?"

"I am still a maniac, but I have not had a violent episode for five years. My logical faculty seems unimpaired, though its exercise has been restricted to the trivial for half a decade."

Gagarin cleared his throat. "That your mental features are *par excellence* is obvious. Your confinement will not be an obstacle as I shall procure everything and everyone you require. I should therefore like to employ your services as a consultant on behalf of His Excellency, Count Brusilov, if you find such an arrangement agreeable."

"I have a question of my own, Captain."

"Yes, sir?"

"I was under the impression that my internment was known only to a small number of government officials, all of them British. How did you find me?"

"The Okhrana."

The Tsar's secret police. I'd always known they'd had agents in London and had never trusted them. "If the commission for Count Brusilov does not run contrary to the interests of my country, then I shall be glad to assist."

"You have my word as an officer and a gentleman that it does not."

"Then perhaps you will sit down and provide me with the relevant details."

Gagarin sat and slapped his hands on his thighs in relief. "Aha! If you will tell me what you already know of the *Demeter*, it will prevent me from revisiting the ground you have already covered."

"Very well. My knowledge stems from the lurid account in the *Dailygraph*, a somewhat more factual one in the *Whitby Gazette*, and a conversation with a coastguard named Skelton. Skelton maintains that the schooner had been floundering off the coast with all sails set for at least two days before the storm and he is something of an expert when it comes to the sea. Regardless, during the storm on Monday night the *Demeter* was blown – or steered – into Whitby harbour, where it ran aground on the stretch of shingle known as Tate Hill Pier, under the East Cliff. The coastguard and police boarded the ship and found it devoid of any crew except the captain, who was dead, and had tied himself to the wheel. There are likely to be some legal complications in the Admiralty Court in relation to salvage for a number of reasons, including the discovery of the tiller in a dead man's hand."

"Your account is most accurate, with the exception of the hound."

"Yes, I read about the giant dog, but didn't pay much heed. What was it supposed to have done... leaped off the ship and flown straight up the sheer East Cliff."

Gagarin frowned. "You do not believe in this hound?"

"It's possible, but I'm afraid you must take tales of black dogs with a pinch of salt in this part of England. The North Riding of Yorkshire is home to the barghest, the most ubiquitous of all of our hell hounds, said to roam from the Dales to the city of York, the coast at Kettleness, and dozens of other places. I'm sure there's something similar in Russian folklore."

"Yes, I see. There is no... *bar-guest*... in my country, but the peasants believe in many evil spirits. The beast in question was, however, corporeal, as it savaged another dog to death later that night."

I pulled on my pipe. "Surely Count Brusilov doesn't want me to find the animal?"

"No, of course not. His Excellency's interest is in the ship's captain, Pyotr Ivanovich Romanov. Captain Romanov is a scion of the great House of Romanov, the family of His Imperial Highness, Tsar Alexander the Third. The relation is a distant one, and Captain Romanov's branch fell into misfortune several generations ago, but His Excellency is determined that his good name be preserved."

"I don't think the count has anything to worry about. Skelton tells me Romanov is being hailed as a hero in Whitby."

Gagarin reached into his reefer jacket and withdrew a sealed envelope. "The inquest was held this morning and the log book examined, in addition to a document Captain Romanov had secured upon his person in a bottle. The log book was in order to August 4th and reported nothing unusual except for the disappearance of the crew. The other document was more... of greater concern. I have made a translation for you. His Excellency returns to London today, but I am to attend Captain Romanov's funeral tomorrow morning and provide you with whatever assistance you require to resolve the mystery."

"Count Brusilov would like the captain's name cleared?"

"His Excellency would like to know the truth, whatever it may be. I have high hopes for Captain Romanov's reputation, but should he have committed a crime—"

"The count would like to be the first to know."

"You have it precisely." Gagarin stood and handed me the envelope. "I shall return after the funeral to take your instructions."

II

On Gagarin's departure, I repaired to the book-closet I had established upstairs, next to my bedchamber. The room was tiny, with a small window affording a view of the houses piled atop each other on the cliff-side, but it was the only one available for use as a study. I removed the contents of the envelope, noted Gagarin's elegant hand, and examined the four sheets of paper at my leisure. Although the pages were clearly an addendum, Romanov had entitled it, *Log of the "Demeter", Varna to Whitby*. It began with a rather ominous sentence: *Written on 18 July, things so strange happening, that I shall keep accurate note henceforth until we land*.

The voyage had started without any such portents, at midday on the 6th July. The captain was accompanied by eight men: two mates, five crew, and a cook. Their freight was recorded as silver sand and boxes of earth. I wondered if this was as remarkable as it seemed and made a memorandum to ask Skelton. On the morning of the 16th July, while the schooner was in the Mediterranean, one of the hands was reported missing. Romanov wrote of a general feeling that someone or *something* was aboard. Sailors the world over are renowned for their superstitions, however, so I set little store by this. Despite dissent from Popescu, his first mate, the captain ordered a thorough search of the ship after one of the crew reported seeing a stranger aboard. Popescu was Roumanian and unpopular with the Russian crew. Nothing was found, though I noted that the boxes of cargo were not opened.

On the 24th July, in the Bay of Biscay, another hand disappeared after going below. Five days later the second mate disappeared and Romanov and Popescu donned side arms as a safeguard. Their precaution was in vain as three more men went missing overnight. According to Romanov, this left only him, Popescu, and two other hands. I went back to the beginning and jotted down the numbers. The captain had evidently made a mistake somewhere, because he had started with eight crew and lost six, which should have left him with Popescu and one Russian hand. He must either have lost only two men on the 29th July or had two remaining. Naturally, he was under extreme stress on the doomed voyage, but the miscalculation seemed unpardonable when it concerned the lives of his crew.

The three – or four – men were having serious problems sailing the schooner, which was now approaching Dover. Romanov had planned to signal for assistance, but was prevented from doing so by inclement weather. At midnight on the 2nd August he responded to a cry from the deck to find Popescu, learning that he had lost another hand. Twenty-four hours later Romanov went to relieve the sole remaining hand, but he was also gone. I scribbled another memorandum and assumed that two rather than three men had gone missing on the 29th July, although Romanov may have been completely unhinged when he wrote the later entries in the addendum – he had already endured so much.

Shortly after Romanov took the helm, Popescu joined him. He was apparently deranged and claimed that he had attacked *It* – presumably the entity responsible for the deaths – with his knife, to no effect. He believed the creature was hiding in the boxes and returned below. Romanov's description of Popescu's insanity seemed to be confirmed by the latter's final actions. He flew from the hatchway, screaming in fear, and cried: He *is here. I know the secret now*. Then he recommended that Romanov join him and threw himself overboard. On the next day, the 4th August, Romanov wrote: *I saw it – him!* He made further reference to *this fiend or monster*, then tied himself to the tiller to make every last effort to bring his vessel safely in to port.

It was one of the most curious narratives I'd ever read, as well as a fascinating puzzle. First, I had to consider not only the accuracy of Gagarin's translation, but also his attention to detail. The secretary's English was almost perfect, but the discrepancy in the numbers of missing crew might have been his mistake rather than Romanov's. Second, if Romanov was a lunatic of some description, I couldn't rely on a single word he'd written. However, the mention of a fiend wasn't necessarily proof of the captain's madness. By the 4th August he was physically, mentally, and morally exhausted, struggling on alone through the bad weather that had dogged the *Demeter* since the Bay of Biscay.

Throughout my career in the police I had relied upon the power of analysis, the science of deduction, and the calculus of probability, those three refinements of absolute logic so essential to the art of detection. Combined with some small skill in observation and a modest breadth of knowledge, my ability to reason had gained me the reputation that had brought Gagarin to my door. Indeed, so strong was my logical synthesis that I had been able to detect my own guilt in the crime which had ended my career, even though I was under the influence of an all-consuming mania, fuelled by alcohol. Now that my sanity and sobriety were restored, I had every hope of succeeding in a commission that fell under my own special province.

I took another look at yesterday's *Dailygraph* and read that Romanov had tied a crucifix and set of prayer beads to his wrist. Although it was illogical to believe in evil spirits, Romanov had taken rational steps to protect himself and made a lucid and courageous decision to save his ship. No matter how sensible an individual Romanov may have been under normal circumstances, his final voyage had been a living hell, aside from which he was a sailor, susceptible to the superstitions of the sea at the best of times. On balance, I was inclined to believe that Romanov was not responsible for the deaths of his crew. He did not strike me as a madman – and I should know. Perhaps that was the count's real reason for employing my services, on the basis of setting a thief to catch a thief rather than my reputation as a police detective.

My cogitations were interrupted by Mrs Knaggs, the housekeeper, delivering the latest *Dailygraph*. The journalist, who went by the unlikely name of Kerr Bostam, was making a meal of his story and had reprinted the entire contents of the captain's addendum by courtesy of an inspector from the Board of Trade. Bostam's own opinion was: *It almost seems as though the captain had been seized with some kind of mania before he had got well into blue water, and this had developed persistently throughout the voyage.* In fairness, he acceded that the public's esteem for the captain was unmitigated. Romanov was to be buried in the graveyard of St Mary's Church, on the East Cliff.

I also noted with annoyance that Bostam made two references to the confounded dog before actually mentioning the verdict of the inquest, which was open. There was nothing about the cause of Romanov's death, which had previously been reported as having occurred within twenty-four hours of his final entries in the log and addendum. Exhaustion or excessive strain to his heart seemed the most likely to me. Meanwhile, the members of Whitby's S.P.C.A. – who obviously had far too much time on their hands – were apparently concerned for the welfare of the mysterious hound, despite the fact that it had ripped open the throat and belly of a large mastiff. At least such was Bostam's implication, the story of the mastiff following close on the heels of the *Demeter's* mascot. The man was in fact relentless, writing of the mourning over the fate of the animal which *would, I believe be adopted by the town*. What utter drivel.

I cast the newspaper down in disgust, refilled my tobacco pouch, and went outside. I found my deck chair exactly where I'd left it on the promenade. A certain restlessness had returned to the sea in my absence and tails of white foam were drifting on the breeze. A few miles to the south, I could see Peak House perched on a cliff. I was in good company for a madman: it was widely held that King George III had been treated there some three quarters of a century ago. I sat and smoked as I considered each possible sequence of events in relation to the evidence available, identifying the limited alternatives and narrowing down the solutions.

By the time the sun set I had constructed a hypothesis from which to work and with which I could present Gagarin. I was also soaked from the salty spray of the sea, which had lately begun to overwhelm the promenade. I carried my chair back to Bay Bow, walked past the Coastguard Station, and entered the Bay Hotel with the intention of finding Skelton.

III

Gagarin arrived at half-past one on Thursday afternoon and our business was once again conducted in the sitting room. From his sombre dress, I gathered he'd come directly from Romanov's funeral. He did not stand on ceremony: "Have you reached a conclusion yet, Mr Langham?"

"No, but I have considered the evidence, and found a number of points that require either clarification or further investigation."

"Please to continue." He withdrew a notebook and a pencil from his coat.

"The man who murdered the crew must be one of Romanov, Popescu, or a stowaway." I paused as Gagarin frowned.

"What about the search on July 16th."

"You evidently know your facts, Captain, but the search did not include the cargo. It is possible that one or more of the boxes was not filled with earth and was used as a hiding place. The boxes were not searched until the 3rd August, when Popescu opened an unspecified number immediately before his demise. I read in the newspaper that the cargo is in the hands of Mr S.F. Billington, a Whitby solicitor. I should like you to exert your influence to find out if it would have been possible for a man to conceal himself in any of these boxes."

He nodded and made a note. "I shall do it."

"I am concerned about the state of Romanov's mind, particularly at the end of the voyage, when he must have been under an incredible amount of physical and psychological stress. I believe his mental state hinges upon one particular point which may be explained by your translation of the addendum." I described the discrepancy in the numbers.

Gagarin made another note. "Unfortunately, I do not have the originals in my possession. The police have retained them pending the Admiralty Court. I shall ask to see them this afternoon. The error may indeed be my own."

"Thank you. I suspect that Romanov *was* in control of his faculties throughout for however irrational his final entry may appear to us in the comfort of this cottage, there can be no doubt his behaviour was appropriate to the situation."

Gagarin leaned forward. "Could you explain this, please?"

"If we accept that Romanov was convinced he had evidence that some kind of murderous evil spirit killed seven of his crew and caused the eighth to commit suicide, then we must conclude that he took the necessary measures to protect himself from the evil and save his ship."

"The evidence of Captain Romanov's rationality... is

his reaction to an evil spirit. You are saying that there *was* an evil spirit?"

"No, I am saying that given the circumstances, it was not unreasonable for a sailor – even an educated one – to believe there was such a thing aboard. In addition to the precautions already described, Romanov even recorded the events in a separate document and took further measures to ensure that this would be available to whoever found the *Demeter*."

"Yes, you are right."

"Let's leave the tired captain for a moment. I would like to speak to a very old sailor named Swales, who may be able to provide me with a more accurate account of the *Demeter's* arrival. I'm told he can usually be found with two of his shipmates in the graveyard on the East Cliff. They sit on a bench above the grave of a gentleman named George Canon."

Gagarin sat up straight and regarded me with disapproval. "This is an English jest, sir?"

"Certainly not. What makes you think so?"

"The man Swales was found dead this morning on the very bench you describe. I learned of it at Captain Romanov's funeral."

"Was he indeed? What was the cause?"

"It is not clear, but I was told he was nearly one hundred years of age. I was also informed that he was found in the seat with his features distorted by a look of utmost fear. There was a curious incident at the funeral, but I suspect it is not significant for it concerns only a dog."

I relented even as I groaned. "Please proceed."

"There was another old sailor sitting on the same bench with two most presentable young ladies. The sailor had brought his dog with him and the animal refused to sit next to them and began howling. It was so loud that it disturbed the priest and eventually the sailor kicked it and dragged it into place, on a gravestone. As soon as the dog reached the grave it stopped howling and started whimpering and shivering. In Russia, the peasants would say that the dog sensed the old man's spirit, which was still restless." He shrugged. "But it is of no consequence."

"I think your peasants might say more than that. George Canon committed suicide in 1873."

Gagarin smiled, for the first time in my presence. "Aha! The grave of a suicide. The peasants say the *upir* lives there."

I shook my head. "What is an *oo-peer*?"

"An un-dead spirit of the Devil. They feed on the blood of men, and often take the form of a wolf. This is an amusing coincidence, yes?"

Perhaps Bostam would have thought so. "While we're on the subject of these bloody hounds – damned and other – I have one more request. I'd like you to check the log of the Demeter to see if there were actually any animals taken aboard by the crew at all." Gagarin made another note. "My final question is about the inquest. Are the authorities completely sure that no one – other than the black dog – left the ship? Bearing in mind the chaos that must have reigned, and the fact that the vessel arrived at night, during one of the worst storms in years."

Gagarin nodded. "I understand your intention. The authorities have completely discounted the possibility. For myself, I also believe it highly unlikely. If that is all, I shall communicate the results of my inquiries as soon as they are complete."

IV

I received Gagarin's answers in a letter delivered by his manservant that evening. Although I was alone in the house, I took the missive up to my book-closet to read.

Sneaton Casle, August 10 1893

My dear Mr Langham

I have the following to report with regard to the Demeter:

1. I have ascertained that of the seventeen boxes of earth opened by Popescu, all were a little over half full and contained enough space for a man to lie in. Furthermore, the lids of all fifty of the boxes have been perforated with small holes, which might allow a man to breathe. The evidence shows, however, that a man would not be able to release the lid from the inside.

2. Please accept my apology for the error in the addendum, which is in fact mine. Captain Romanov reported two disappearances on the night of July 29th, not three.

3. The ship's log does not report any live animals taken on board for the voyage.

His Excellency has recalled me to London, but any further assistance you may require can be procured from Mr S.F. Billington of Billington & Son, No.7 The Crescent, Whitby, who has been retained by me for this purpose. May I ask that you dispatch the results of your investigation to me at the embassy in Chesham Place.

I remain, My dear Sir, Yours sincerely,

Vladimir Iosifovich Gagarin.

I suspected that I now had all the facts which I was likely to acquire at my disposal. I also had a premonition that the conclusion which must logically follow the premises I'd established would be disturbing. Maybe even paradoxical. As I sat back in my wicker chair, I heard the crashing of the waves against the sea wall below, a reminder of the opaque nightmares that had haunted my dreams before, during, and after the tempest. The breakers hurled themselves against the fragile stone and mortar as aberrant thoughts assailed my mind with equal vigour. I tried to keep my overactive imagination at bay by concentrating on my analytical skills.

Who murdered the Russian sailors?

I was prepared to discount Romanov, which left either Popescu or an unknown individual. In the latter instance, the culprit was required to have hidden in a box for ten days, opened it by means unknown, picked off the entire crew one by one even though they were alert to his presence, and then escaped undetected when the schooner ran aground. The offender must also necessarily have had suicidal tendencies to continue killing the crew in the ferocious weather. Homicidal mania itself was inconsistent with the sustained and calculated manner with which the crew had been despatched and discovery avoided. On reflection, I was inclined to regard the possibility of a stowaway as not only implausible, but absurd. My experiences as a detective had repeatedly taught me that the simplest explanation was invariably the most sound. There was thus no need to posit an unknown entity for which there was so little evidence when the facts appeared to incriminate Popescu.

I went through my hypothesis again, and once more arrived at Popescu as by far the most likely culprit. I picked up my fountain pen to communicate the same to Gagarin, but stopped.

I laughed to myself.

Popescu was the most likely of my three suspects, but what if I included a fourth, an evil spirit of sorts like Gagarin's fairy tale shapechanger? I had already decided Romanov was sane. Perhaps Popescu was as well. If he *was* a murderer, driven by bloodthirsty xenophobia, why didn't he kill his captain? Romanov was no ordinary Russian, he was related to the nation's ruling family. The existence of a malevolent spirit actually fitted the facts of the case far better than a homicidal Popescu.

I laughed again, tittering uncontrollably – I couldn't help it.

The only illogical aspect of selecting the shapechanger over Popescu was the supernatural quality of the creature itself. I felt like Romanov tying himself to his doomed tiller as I reconsidered my explanation. Cast in this new, otherworldly light, everything described in the addendum made sense... and not just the incidents aboard the *Demeter*: the immense dog that leaped up the East Cliff, the coalman's dead dog, the dog on the suicide's grave, and maybe even old Swales.

That night I dreamed of barghests, dogs, hell hounds, and wolves.

V

Robin Hood's Bay, Aug.11. 1893

My Dear Sir

I have the honour to present my findings following my investigation into the deaths of Captain Romanov and the crew of the Demeter.

I believe Captain Romanov had the misfortune to take on board a fiend of some sort, exactly as he described in the final entry of the addendum. I am unable to ascertain any particulars of the creature, except that it appears to have left the ship in the form of a giant dog and now reposes in the resting place of Mr George Canon, in the graveyard of St Mary's Church, in Whitby.

With the assurance of my high esteem and my appreciation of your own sterling efforts and assistance with regard to the case, I am, Captain Gagarin,

Very sincerely yours,

Roderick Langham.

I couldn't write that, could I?

If Brusilov took offence he'd have me back in a straitjacket in Scarborough before Caine could place his next bet. I probably deserved such a fate, but couldn't face it. The second paragraph of the letter I sent read:

Although it is likely to be impossible to verify the tragic events with complete certainty, I believe it is beyond a reasonable doubt that the first mate Popescu murdered the crew and then committed suicide in the early hours of the 4th August, exactly as surmised by Captain Romanov in the addendum.

VI

The rain stopped shortly before dusk on Friday so I took my pipe out to the promenade. I was faced with a dreadful dilemma. Either I had completely lost my reason years ago and could never be sure of myself again, or my morality was once more in question. I had deliberately presented Popescu as the villain of the piece. He may not have been a popular chap, but I think he was as brave as Romanov. He had first sought the evil out and then chosen a sailor's end over death at the hands of the Devil. Six years ago I had murdered an innocent man; now I had assassinated the character of an honourable one. Was there no end to my iniquity? I hoped Popescu had no kith and kin to be deceived by my lie, but even if he didn't, no man deserved to have his reputation besmirched in so brutal a fashion, let alone a brave man, and by a moral coward of dubious sanity.

I leaned against the rusted railing as I smoked, my hand trembling.

It could not be. If I *had* lost my reason, then my speculation about the shapechanger was invalid. There was no such thing as a shapechanger outside of fairy tales and Gothic romances so I must be mad to conclude the existence of one. And if I was a maniac, then so was Popescu, homicidal where I was fanciful. For the first time in my wretched life I wanted to be mad, for if I was irrational all was well with the world. If my reason was intact, however, not only was I a coward, but the cosmic consequences were too horrible to contemplate. I *must* be a maniac... there were *no* shapechangers, *no* barghests, *no* Devils.

Suddenly, I sensed someone at my side.

I drew back form the railing and turned to see a tall, thin man with an aquiline nose and grey moustache. He stood mere inches away from me though I had not heard his approach. In the moonlight, his cruel face was so pale that I could see the veins underneath the skin. There was a scar on his forehead and his eyes looked as red as his thick, sensuous lips.

My jaw dropped open and my pipe fell from my mouth, breaking on the wet stone. I stared for a moment before regaining control.

The instant I closed my mouth he opened his. His nostrils dilated and he revealed large, white teeth, pointed like those of a beast. I didn't see him move, but felt the vice of his ice cold hand close on my throat. His grip was as strong as that of twenty men and I knew I was completely at his mercy. I froze in fear, losing control of my physical faculties. The fiend's hand locked against my jaw and he lifted me two feet from the ground in a single, swift motion.

I hung there petrified, suspended in the air by the hand of a dead man. He held all of my thirteen stone without any sign of strain and even relaxed his grip enough to allow the blood to flow to my brain. I grimaced at his breath. It was like the smell of everything that had ever died – the ancient, the old, and the recently rotting – wafting into my mouth and up my nose. After what seemed like an eternity, he spoke in an accent from the Balkan reaches of the Austro-Hungarian Empire.

"You know who I am?"

I couldn't reply, but I tried to nod.

"The meaner things obey me and sense my approach. Dogs and madmen. You have told the English about me, the Russians?"

I attempted to shake my head, then let go of his arms and waved to plead my innocence.

"I do not believe you." He snarled and swung me through the air.

He was going to throw me into the sea. I clung to his arm for dear life, but he cast me onto the walkway instead. Sprawled across the stone and quavering in terror, I squinted up at him, my teeth clamped, face rigid.

He smiled. "But your friends will not believe you either and there has already been too much death in this place when I have many labours left."

He raised his arm and I had not the courage to watch my own slaughter.

The *coup de grâce* never came.

When I forced my eyes to open he was gone.

I stumbled back to Bay Bow and ransacked the rooms until I found one of McGinty's caches of gin.

For the first time in many years I drank myself into oblivion.

5. The Wrong Doctor

A literary adventure

"When a doctor goes wrong he is the first of criminals. He has nerve and he has knowledge."

Sherlock Holmes, 1883

I

Baker Street, London

My dear Mr Langham – I am sure that you wish to forget the unfortunate circumstances of your meeting with Mr Holmes and I, but I nonetheless beg your indulgence. Holmes' intervention in the Windover Hill affair was motivated by the pursuit of justice and I suspect that your preference, as an agent of the law, was for the prevention of further offences. In this regard, I was pleased to discover that you have been living peacefully on the Yorkshire coast these last fifteen years. If you are able to accommodate a brief interruption of your retirement, I would esteem it a great kindness if you would favour me with your opinion on a criminal matter in which I am unable to consult Mr Holmes. I shall call upon you at 4pm on Thursday. I shall try again at the same time on Friday. In the event that neither is convenient, I shall await you in the Royal Hotel, where I have reserved a room for the duration of the weekend.

Yours sincerely
John H. Watson
March 25th 1902

I was surprised at the letter, but not at the skill with
which Watson piqued my curiosity. He was, of course,
something of a polymath – a doctor, a soldier, a
detective, and lately a man of letters – and in this
respect much more like Holmes than the self-
deprecating tone of his memoirs revealed. He
exemplified, in matter of fact, the ideal to which all
gentlemen in the British Empire should aspire even if
so many of us fall short of it.

My own fall had been administered by Holmes
when he had discovered my homicidal
somnambulism, an unfortunate symptom of a hitherto
unknown kind of dementia which resulted in me
investigating a crime I had myself committed. My
health and fortune had both taken several turns since
and I was now head of a modest household in Whitby.
I supported myself, my housekeeper (the aptly-named
Mrs Knaggs), and her young son with the anonymous
scribbling of the implausible adventures of *the other
Baker Street* detective, the fictional – and rather
ridiculous – Sexton Blake.

Watson's letter was part of a parcel that arrived in
the last post on Wednesday, the remainder of which
was a thick octavo volume entitled *The Hound of the
Baskervilles*. The latest of Holmes' adventures had
begun in the *Strand* the previous summer and the
penultimate instalment was still on my desk. I was
grateful for the gift, which would allow me to finish
the tale before the April issue of the magazine arrived,
but it was a strange choice. My identity as a Sexton
Blake author was known only to my editor and Watson
could not have guessed that I was an enthusiastic
member of his reading public when all the evidence –

my status as a victim of Holmes' scientific method – pointed in the opposite direction.

I set the letter aside, opened the novel, and flipped through the pages. The book contained full-page plates of all of Mr Paget's wonderful illustrations, but I ceased my perusal as I neared the end. I reached for the March *Strand*, numbered 135 in volume xxiii, where the instalment ended in high dramatic style, part-way through chapter fourteen, with the emergence of the hound "out of the wall of fog". I noted that on the previous page I had underlined Holmes comment to Watson on this meteorological phenomenon with a pencil: *Very serious indeed – the one thing upon earth which could have disarranged my plans.* By the time I finished Watson's novel, I knew precisely why he would be calling at No. 10 Flowergate the following afternoon.

II

Watson knocked while the clock was striking four and I opened the door promptly. He had changed very little since our one and only meeting and was an altogether fine specimen of a man our age – for we were both close upon our half-centuries. He was still athletic in build, maintained a military bearing, and continued to wear his handkerchief in his sleeve. The only difference I could discern were the streaks of grey in his moustache and I reflected that while I was but a shadow of my former self, Watson had remained the quintessential English gentleman. As host, the overture was mine to make.

"Good day, Dr Watson, how do you do?"

He smiled, removed his right glove, and took my hand in a firm, honest grip. "Very well, thank you, Mr Langham. You too appear to be in excellent health."

"Pray come in. Allow me to take your stick and coat. The sideboard will support the weight of your hat and gloves admirably." I ushered him into my sitting-room, where the fire was keeping the cold at bay. "Do sit down and make yourself comfortable. I have asked Mrs Knaggs to make tea. May I offer you some?"

Watson's limp was slightly more pronounced than I remembered, though he walked quite steadily without his stick. "Yes, please, that's very kind of you." I rang the bell on the side-table, imagined rather than heard the corresponding grunt of disapproval in the kitchen, and sat down with less ease than Watson. He glanced at the copy of *The Hound*, which I had placed on a footstool. "May I also thank you for your kindness in receiving me today. I trust that my presence is not inconvenient."

"Not at all." Holmes impressed his clients by deducing facts about them from their appearance and mannerisms and I was determined to entertain Watson with an equivalent performance. I lifted the volume for effect. "Mr Holmes as represented in this gripping tale of yours is not quite the man I met in Sussex the previous year. He is, if I may say so, not at his best."

Watson betrayed no emotion, but asked, "What evidence leads you to that conclusion?"

"There are several points, but one is conclusive." I quoted without opening the book: "*The one thing upon earth which could have disarranged my plans.* What native Briton would be surprised by the sudden appearance of fog on Dartmoor? Common sense aside, Mr Holmes had both visited the moor during the Straker investigation and spent several days and nights on the tor. Furthermore, he had motive to exercise extra care in making his final plans given his earlier failure to safeguard his client's life – I refer, of course, to Selden's death. In sum, Dr Watson, Sherlock Holmes was wrong!"

I let the volume fall on the footstool, but the drama in my *dénouement* was ruined by Mrs Knaggs, who waddled in with a wide tray loaded with tea, biscuits, and custard tartlets. She greeted Watson with enthusiasm – he was still, of course, a handsome man much-beloved by the fair sex – placed the tray on the table with uncharacteristic care, and even uttered a gracious "thank you, sir" when I said I would serve my guest. Watson indicated his preferences for milk, no sugar, and biscuits, then waited for me to resume my seat.

"You are correct, Mr Langham. Holmes had not yet recovered from his physical breakdown in Lyon in eighty-seven and was on the verge of a mental one when I'm afraid to admit that I abandoned him for my late wife." Watson's face contorted with pain for a moment. "Eighty-eight was also the first occasion on which he crossed swords with Professor Moriarty, and whatever other work he was engaged upon, he was always also unravelling Moriarty's web."

I seized on the mention of Moriarty for my second *dénouement*: "It is no coincidence that you decided to consult me when I happen to reside some fifty miles from an assassin with whom I myself crossed swords during my police career." I leaned forward and picked up *The Hound* again. "Moriarty was the man behind the attacks on the Baskerville family and Moran was his agent. Colonel Sebastian Moran, lately retired to the Grange in the Yorkshire Dales, is the real killer of the Baskervilles!"

Watson shook his head. "No, not Moriarty or Moran, Mortimer."

My shock rapidly gave way to horror and I opened the novel to the first page of the final chapter: *Sir Henry and Dr Mortimer were, however, in London, on*

their way to that long voyage which had been
recommended for the restoration of his shattered
nerves. "Sir Henry's voyage with Dr Mortimer!"

Watson continued to shake his head. "A sabbatical from which he never returned."

III

Now that I'd been told, it seemed not only the obvious, but the inevitable, conclusion to the narrative. "You left clues, didn't you? The adversarial nature of Mortimer's first meeting with Holmes, Holmes' recognition of his scientific acumen, Mortimer's position as executor of Sir Charles' estate, his defensiveness when questioned about the will, his apparent willingness to believe the legend..."

"I wrote some drivel about an unseen force entangling us in an imperceptible net, but it was true. It was Mortimer. He was always *there*. Everywhere! It began with the ruse with the stick to put us off guard and finished with him dragging Sir Henry off to sea. Mortimer introduced us to first the legend and then Sir Henry, he never left Sir Henry's side in London, and he visited Sir Henry and I every day at Baskerville Hall. He shepherded the young baronet to his death and stage-managed Holmes, Stapleton, the whole damned case. I told Holmes of my suspicions, but he wouldn't believe it."

"The missing page from your letters!" I cried.

"Yes."

I knew I was caught up in the thrill of it all, so I forced myself to adopt an analytic approach, probing for weaknesses. "But what about Stapleton – and his wife's statement?"

"Rodger Baskerville was a bloody fool. Holmes couldn't account for his plan because he didn't have one. He disgraced himself as Baskerville in Costa Rica and Vandeleur in Pickering and I think his arrival in Dartmoor was a sign of desperation. He was the perfect foil for Mortimer."

"I thought it was odd that Holmes' description of *a foil as quick and supple as my own* ended up referring to such a bungler. Why did his wife implicate him if he wasn't guilty – good God, Mortimer was having an affair with her, wasn't he!"

"You are most perceptive, Mr Langham. Mortimer told us that his wife was an invalid, but he was in fact a widower. Mrs Beryl Baskerville was tired of being dragged around the world by her petty criminal of a husband and appears to have been easy prey for Mortimer. It's not enough to cover one's tracks, one needs to offer an alternative suspect to the authorities and who better than Stapleton? I don't know exactly what transpired at Merripit House after Sir Henry left, but I do know that Mortimer was waiting for Stapleton on the moor."

I wasn't convinced yet. "But the Baskerville case was about securing the fortune. Surely Sir Henry wasn't foolish enough to leave it to a gentleman he had just met?"

"I am not presenting my conjecture clearly. Mortimer was in league with Mr James Desmond, Sir Henry's cousin."

"Ah, I thought he was dismissed rather too quickly by Holmes. An elderly clergyman or some such?"

"The *late* Mr Desmond was retired from the pulpit, infirm and reclusive. Holmes eliminated him as a suspect on the basis of a telegram from the Westmoreland constabulary and nothing else. He was, as you have said, far from his best."

"Mortimer killed Desmond?"

Watson enumerated Mortimer's crimes on his fingers. "Mortimer murdered Sir Charles, Stapleton,

Sir Henry, and then Desmond. The first and last death were attributed to natural causes and the second and third involved disappearances in circumstances where it was impossible to recover the corpses. Mortimer was Desmond's sole beneficiary. He committed four perfect crimes and secured a fortune of close to three quarters of a million pounds."

A man with less charisma than Watson could have persuaded me to accept his theory: the re-solution concealed in the text of the novel was a great deal more plausible than the purported solution. "How may I be of assistance?" I asked.

"I am shortly to abandon Holmes for a second time and I should like to bring the matter to a close beforehand by way of compensation. I intend to confront Mortimer tomorrow morning and would very much appreciate your company."

"Then I'd better pack." I reached for the bell.

"There's no need. Mortimer used his ill-gotten gains to build himself a manor house on the North York Moors. Would you believe he lives on the edge of *Howl* Moor? If I put that in a memoir I'd be accused of writing fiction."

"What brought him here, the archaeology?"

"Possibly, but more likely his wife's bidding. The ghost of Mrs Vandeleur has returned to her old haunt disguised as Mrs Mortimer."

IV

Watson and I boarded the first train for York on Friday morning and arrived in the little village of Goathland fifteen minutes later. The station-master directed us to the inn-keeper, who offered us a sturdy wagonette, for although our destination was only a few miles hence, the road was poor. Watson declined the offer of a driver, took the reins himself, and moved over so that I could join him. He seemed to know where he was going and we set off into a bright but chilly morning, the surrounding mist gradually yielding to the combination of sunshine and a stiff breeze from the west. The track upon which we travelled traversed the gentle slope of the moorland, rising to our right and subsiding to our left. Both sides were dominated by the bright purple of the heather rather than the darker greens and browns of the grass and shrubs. Aside from the distant ridge from which the wind fell and a small forest a mile or more away, the horizontal expanse was punctuated only by a few black-faced sheep and the occasional dry-stone wall.

I had spent Thursday evening consulting the records of the Whitby Literary and Philosophical Society, of which I was a member, and committed a large-scale map of the north-eastern quarter of the moors to memory. Hunters Hall was located between Hazel Wood and Grey Earths Wood to the north and Wade's Causeway and Howl Moor to the south. Mortimer had already made his mark on the moors by clearing the causeway of vegetation and had published papers to the effect that the landmark was a Roman road. He was no doubt in search of skulls – skulls which he had apparently been depositing in, as well as removing from, the earth. Watson kept his own counsel throughout our journey and I was not altogether certain of the reason for my presence. My guess was that I was a deterrent in the event that Mortimer decided to add a fresh corpse to the Neolithic and Bronze Age skeletons beneath the causeway, but maybe there was more to it.

Shortly after passing Grey Earths Wood, we turned south onto a narrower track that curved around a rock-strewn rise before ending in a line of rowans, twisted and bent by centuries of storm and wind. A tall, narrow tower rose above the trees. Watson pointed with the whip. "Hunters Hall."

We approached an ugly ironstone lodge, squatting next to a pair of shiny wrought-iron gates. The gates were open and there was no sign of life in the lodge. The avenue beyond was deep in shadow, bending sharply out of sight after a few dozen yards. In the shade, hard and clear like an equestrian statue upon its pedestal, was a mounted man. He was sombre and stern, a penang-lawyer poised over his forearm as he watched the path of our approach.

"Watson," I whispered, but he was already halting the horses.

The rider emerged from the gloom. "Well, if it isn't Mr Sherlock Holmes and Dr Watson."

I recognised James Mortimer M.R.C.S. from Watson's thumb-nail sketch in *The Hound*. His height, emaciation, protruding nose, and bowed back combined to give the impression of a human sickle perched precariously on a horse's back. He was wearing an expensive broad-brimmed hat, gold-rimmed spectacles, and a smart silk cravat, but his attire deteriorated as it descended: a shabby frock-coat, creased trousers, and muddy riding boots. He had not lost the air of peering benevolence with which Watson had characterised him and indeed he thrust his head at us as if to bring his close-set eyes nearer to their target.

"I've been expecting you gentlemen for a very long time. I thought I'd been granted a reprieve when Mr Holmes' demise was reported, but when I heard you'd survived I was sure you'd find your way here. When Beryl told me about the publication in the *Strand* in August, I awaited you each evening. Now, I must – hallo, you're not Mr Holmes! Who's this, Dr Watson?"

"My associate, Mr Roderick Langham. Mr Langham,

Dr James Mortimer. Why were you expecting Holmes and I?"

"Because sooner or later it must have dawned on Mr Holmes that he was wrong. If Sir Henry's disappearance at sea wasn't obvious enough, the brevity of the period Mr Desmond's god granted him to enjoy his fortune must have made my position plain." Mortimer was neither fearful nor contemptuous as he all but admitted his guilt.

"You murdered both Baskervilles, Stapleton, and Desmond." There was ice in Watson's voice.

"Morally, I am responsible. Legally... I'm not going to insult your intelligence by pointing out the public facts of two deaths by natural causes, one by misadventure, and one by suicide."

"You gloat, sir."

"I am a man of science, Doctor, I deal solely in facts and leave others to pass judgement."

"I assure you I am here for that very purpose. I am well-acquainted with the facts and I intend to share every last detail of my judgement with you. I may not have proof that will stand in a court of law, but you will not sleep soundly from this day forward."

"No, sir, no, you are in error. Hiring Mr Holmes gave me a credibility with Sir Henry which I could never have gained otherwise, but it was always a calculated risk. The reappearance of Mr Holmes at some later date was a part of that risk so I have been prepared for this day for many years. To be perfectly frank, I am relieved that the moment has arrived at last and I feel that you have done me a service, even if that was not your intention. I should like to repay that service. You are seeking some sense of an ending, something akin to that with which you complete the stories my wife admires so? As long as this gentleman," he rotated his head towards me, "has no official standing, I shall be glad to receive you both tomorrow evening and answer any questions that lie between us. Say five o'clock? Very good. Now that's settled, would you be so kind as to remove your conveyance from my gateway. There is just enough room for you to manoeuvre without having to enter."

V

Watson asked if I would mind postponing discussion until we had returned to Whitby, so I spent the journey back by wagonette, train, and foot smoking my pipe in silent contemplation. I could not fathom Mortimer, who seemed as cool a customer as any criminal I had ever faced in my day. My main concern was Watson. What would he do? He had maintained a steely calm throughout the interview and an immobility and impenetrability of countenance worthy of Holmes since, but what could he hope to achieve? Mortimer had committed the most perfect series of murders imaginable. Even the circumstantial evidence was severely limited and if Mortimer was able to prove prior acquaintance with Desmond, then that too would evaporate like the mist. If Watson wasn't careful, he might find himself embroiled in a libel battle with an extremely wealthy man, in the process of which Holmes' reputation would be torn to shreds by the press. A glance at my acquaintance's fine, noble features nonetheless gave me confidence in his ability to find a solution to the problem.

Midday found us back in my sitting-room, drinking tea while Mrs Knaggs prepared luncheon upstairs.

"Now that we have both had sufficient time to mull this conundrum over, may I enquire as to your thoughts?"

I cleared my throat. "I must disappoint you, for I see only danger ahead."

"So do I. Holmes once said *when a doctor goes wrong he is the first of criminals; he has nerve and he has knowledge.* Mortimer's nerve enabled him to do away with the two younger gentlemen with the utmost efficacy; his knowledge enabled him to take advantage of the older gentlemen's respective medical conditions. I have seen many cases with a great deal more evidence fail to reach the courtroom."

"Were I still a detective, I would not embarrass myself by presenting the case to the Director of Public Prosecutions as-is. The only way I can see that changing is if Mortimer's wife can be persuaded to testify against him and now that we're discussing the matter, I wonder if we placed her in danger this morning."

Watson's brow furrowed and he scratched his head. "I think that you're right about Mrs Mortimer being the only witness, but then again, how much has she actually witnessed? She will have known something of Mortimer's machinations on the moor, but I doubt she was privy to much more. He would only have confided in her completely if his trust was total, in which case she will not stand witness. If, on the other hand, she knows as little as I suspect, she would be no good on the witness stand. Either way, I think Mrs Mortimer safe."

I nodded. "And we mustn't let chivalry or prejudice against the weaker sex blind us to the fact that Beryl Garcia has chosen to spend all of her adult life with criminal husbands. Furthermore, the performance you describe at the end of *The Hound* was quite obviously just that, a performance. What do you intend to do?"

"I am afraid that I cannot answer that question, but I would be very grateful for your company tomorrow evening."

"You may count on it."

"I am indebted, sir, thank you."

"If Mrs Mortimer doesn't join us, perhaps you could slip away and seek a private interview with her. I could always distract Mortimer with talk of Bertillon or Lombroso."

Watson fixed me with a grave stare, the meaning of which was far from clear. Eventually, he said, "I think Lombroso would be more to his taste."

"I don't read Italian, but I have several of his papers from *The Monist* in my library. I shall spend tomorrow brushing up on them!"

Once again, I had predicted Watson's intentions. He was going to turn that gentlemanly charm which had so impressed ladies on three continents to a lady from a fourth. I wondered if he had perhaps been more intimate with the then Beryl Stapleton than he had revealed in the memoir. It mattered little. I was convinced that Watson would succeed and determined to assist him in any way possible.

VI

Watson and I crossed the threshold of Hunters Hall at a few minutes after five on Saturday evening. He had opted to hire a driver this time, so we were both sitting comfortably in the back as the wagonette clattered along the avenue. Though the sun was far from setting, the day was overcast and the canopy formed by the trees clutching at each other low over our heads contributed to the gloom. The dark tunnel soon opened onto a broad turf lawn and we saw the hall for the first time. The building was a huge basalt block, with a porch projecting to the front and a single steeple rising high above us. The steeple was surrounded by four great chimneys, three of which puffed grey smoke into a greyer sky. The antique style, augmented with mullioned windows and copious amounts of ivy, was at odds with the pristine stone, but the cheerful freshness made a welcome change from the sinister gateway. We were met by a smartly-dressed footman, who led us up the stairs into a modern entrance hall raftered with baulks of timber and decorated with innocuous paintings of rural and pastoral scenes. Watson appeared to pay the hall careful attention as the butler took our hats, coats, sticks, and gloves. I suspected he was familiarising himself with the floor-plan in the event that he found himself alone. We were directed from the hall to a parlour with cream and blue décor, a high vault, and fashionable clutter.

Mortimer was warming his hands by the fire, dressed much the same as the previous day. He turned to us. "Good evening, gentlemen. May I offer you some refreshment... tea, coffee, something a little stronger?"

"Just privacy, Dr Mortimer – unless Mrs Mortimer is joining us, of course."

"No, Doctor, Mrs Mortimer has no desire to renew your acquaintance. That will be all, Soames, please make sure I am not disturbed."

The butler left, closing the door behind him.

"Now, you must excuse my attire, but I've only just returned from the moors. I'm rather busy at present, with two excavations in addition to the work on what I can safely call Wheeldale Road. Please make yourselves at home."

There were four armchairs and a settle arranged around a long, low table atop which sat a large silver tray and cloche, a battered old cigarette case, and a leather tobacco pouch. Mortimer favoured the settle and Watson and I sat facing him. There was a second door behind Mortimer, which would be useful if Watson had to slip out undetected.

Mortimer peered over the table at us. "I hope you don't mind, but I've invited Stapleton to join us."

Watson kept his cool, but I couldn't help myself. "*Stapleton*?"

"Well, no, 'Stapleton' was one of his many aliases; Rodger Baskerville is his real name."

I turned to Watson, then back to Mortimer. "If Baskerville is alive, then your marriage to his wife is null and void."

Mortimer smiled. "I didn't say he was alive." He leaned forward, removed the cloche, and revealed a perfectly preserved skull.

I gasped. Not because of the skull or the surgical implications of its presence on the tray, but because of the legal use to which it could be put. It was all we needed. If Watson had brought his service revolver along we could simply seize it at gunpoint and make good our escape. I turned to him again, but he was staring at Mortimer.

Mortimer laughed. "Do forgive my little jest, but I admit it was worth it. If you could have seen your faces! This is the skull of the man you knew as Jack Stapleton, Dr Watson. You may note that it bears a remarkably similar supra-orbital development to that of Mr Holmes. Unfortunately in Baskerville's case it was not an indication of intellect, for the man blundered from one disaster to the next like one of his hapless butterflies. There were two scandals in South America, not one, then the school in Pickering and finally the fiasco on Dartmoor. I allowed him to flit about in my net until Mr Holmes skewered him with the blame and then I with something more substantial. Let me remove my *memento mori* so we are not distracted." Mortimer returned the cloche to its place, stood, picked up the tray, and stepped over to the sideboard. "As I am acquainted with the nature of your quest let me say that I shall be telling you that which I have not and will not confide to anyone else."

Watson flashed a glance at the windows flanking

the sideboard, then at both doors, and then at me. He raised his left hand, indicating I should stay seated.

I nodded.

Watson rose, and moved in behind Mortimer.

I knew he was capable of dealing with our host, so I decided to grab the skull and make for the wagonette if a struggle ensued.

Mortimer set down the tray. "But where is Mr Holmes?" The low clang of metal on wood was muffled by a sharp click, a sound that I hadn't heard in a while, but recognised instantly. Mortimer turned as Watson raised his right hand from his pocket.

Mortimer's mouth dropped open and Watson shot him through the forehead; flesh, blood, and brain matter spattering sideboard, curtains, and window.

Watson turned, clutching the smoking revolver in his fist, and I jumped up, grabbing hold of my chair.

He marched towards me, kicked his chair over, reached down to edge of the table, and flung it on its side. Then he faced me, cocked the revolver again, and lifted it.

He was going to kill me too, blame Mortimer's murder on me.

In the fraction of a second I hesitated, Watson pressed the barrel to his left thigh and fired.

There was more smoke and more blood.

He cried out, dropped the weapon, and fell to the floor.

"I'm sorry, Langham, but this has always been my intention. I couldn't let Mortimer escape unpunished any more than I could let Holmes' good name be destroyed. We are all in your hands now."

VII

I do not know if my decision to bear false witness for

Watson has redeemed my past or damned my future, but I do know that I could not let him throw his life away for the likes of Mortimer. Watson committed murder to defend his friend's reputation and I committed perjury to defend his, and the reputation of the English gentleman which he epitomised for me and so many others. He had nerve and he had knowledge.

6. The Paradol Chamber

A scientific adventure

"The unit of this scale was chosen arbitrarily as the sum of two just noticeable differences, and the term 'dol' was suggested as the name of the unit of pain intensity."

Studies on Pain: An Investigation of Some Quantitative Aspects of the Dol Scale of Pain Intensity,

Hardy, Wolff & Goodell, 1947

I

The Grange, West Burton

My dear Mr Langham – I trust you will forgive the impertinence of this interruption of your retirement, but I am a direct man by nature. I have reason to believe that although we may have been at odds with one another in the distant past, we have both been done a great disservice by Mr. Sherlock Holmes. In this regard, I think you will be interested in the intelligence I have concerning Holmes' involvement in the Whitechapel case and in a proposal I should like to put to you. I shall

call upon you at 9am on Thursday. If convenient,
please inform me by return of post.

Yours sincerely

Sebastian R. Moran

October 5ᵗʰ 1903

I was startled by the missive, which was full of
surprises despite its succinctness. The first was the
timing. The October *Strand*, numbered 154 in volume
xxvi, lay on my desk, having arrived on Friday. The
frontispiece comprised a picture of my correspondent
locked in a struggle for his freedom drawn by Mr
Paget, which served to introduce the first episode of
The Return of Sherlock Holmes, entitled 'The
Adventure of the Empty House'. Human beings are apt
to impose patterns where they do not exist and
detectives – professional, retired, or amateur – are
consequently guilty of ascribing causation to
coincidence, but I nonetheless very much doubted this
was a coincidence. Watson's popular decision to
resume publication of his tales had itself coincided
with Holmes' controversial decision to retire at the age
of forty-nine and the former was very likely a direct
consequence of the latter. The second surprise was
that Colonel Moran knew where to find me. My home
in the little port of Whitby, on the edge of the North
York Moors, was only fifty-odd miles from his on the
eastern edge of the Yorkshire Dales, but I had taken
pains to ensure that my retirement remained
undisturbed.

Then there was the letter's content. After a brief and
unhappy service in the Indian Army I had spent a
decade in the Metropolitan Police Force. Holmes had
detected my homicidal somnambulism, an
unfortunate symptom of a hitherto unknown kind of
dementia that resulted in me investigating a crime I

had myself unwittingly committed. My health and
fortune had both taken several turns since, until I
became head of the modest household at No.10
Flowergate. I supported myself, my housekeeper, and
her young son with the anonymous scribbling of the
implausible adventures of *the other Baker Street*
detective, the fictional – and rather ridiculous –
Sexton Blake. Like all writers and readers of detective
fiction, I was familiar with the public facts of the
Whitechapel murders. Unlike those writers and
readers, I was also privy to a number of private facts.
Holmes' discovery of my guilt had been a potential
cause for great embarrassment to the Metropolitan
Police and instead of being tried in a court of law I was
placed under what should have been indefinite house
arrest in a remote fishing village. My last jailer was a
gross, alcoholic young Munsterman by the name of
McGinty whose first case on being appointed a
detective had been the Whitechapel murders. They
had clearly disturbed him deeply and he talked about
them incessantly as he drank himself to death.

I put down Moran's letter and picked up the *Strand*,
flicking through to page three hundred and seventy-
four. In his narrative, Watson had quoted the
following passage from Holmes' index of biographies:

Moran, Sebastian, Colonel. Unemployed. *Formerly
1st Bangalore Pioneers. Born London, 1840. Son of Sir
Augustus Moran, C. B., once British Minister to Persia.
Educated Eton and Oxford. Served in Jowaki Campaign,
Afghan Campaign, Charasiab (despatches), Sherpur,
and Cabul. Author of* Heavy Game of the Western
Himalayas, *1881;* Three Months in the Jungle, *1884.
Address: Conduit Street. Clubs: The Anglo-Indian, the
Tankerville, the Bagatelle Card Club.*

I wasn't sure if I knew more about Moran than
Watson or if he had deliberately altered information
for poetic or moral reasons, but the sketch was not

entirely accurate. For one, both Moran's parentage and place of birth were disputed and it was widely believed that he had been adopted by Sir Augustus. Second, Moran was a brevet lieutenant colonel, although he was of course addressed as colonel out of courtesy. Third, the last regiment in which he had served had been changed, no doubt to protect its reputation. Finally, Watson had abbreviated Moran's military service, which included Bhutan, the Zululand Campaign, and a second mention-in-despatches at Kandahar. He had resigned his commission in order to devote more time to hunting and writing at the end of 1880, but had apparently tired of the former, returning to the comforts of London after a couple of years. He had not been back very long when he had been recruited by Moriarty and turned to the hunting of that most dangerous of animals. Watson's latest tale told of Moran's arrest for the murder of the Honourable Ronald Adair in 1894, facilitated by Holmes, after which he had been convicted. Watson had, however, omitted the most interesting aspect of the whole affair: Moran had been released from Holloway fifteen months into his sentence on the grounds of ill health and then – for reasons shrouded in secrecy – received an official pardon the following year. He had withdrawn from the public eye since. Moran's letter had arrived with the first post on Tuesday, which allowed me more than enough time to reply. I reached for my writing utensils immediately.

II

Though I cared little for my own life, I despatched both Mrs Knaggs and her son on an early errand to the market in Pickering in order to prevent them from being victims of, or witness to, any mischief Moran may have had in mind. I also posted Moran's letter and a copy of my reply to him to myself shortly after my household had decamped to the train station so that any investigation into that mischief might not prove too taxing for the police. I brewed a pot of tea and a pot of coffee, tended to the fire, and flicked through the first copy of the new series of the *Union Jack*, the latest venue for the lucrative twaddle that flowed so freely from my pen. Two minutes after the clock struck nine, I heard three loud raps on the front door. Moran was now sixty-three, a dozen years my senior, and from the description and depiction in the *Strand* I was expecting him to be tall, portly, and white-whiskered. The man who stood before me was in fact of medium height, slim, with a full head of thinning hair and a neat, grey moustache. He had a deeply tanned and lined face, a hawk nose, and hooded eyes. I was reminded of someone else I had seen in a magazine, although I could not put a name to the face.

"Good day, Colonel Moran, how do you do?" I did not offer my hand and neither did he.

"A pleasure to meet you, Mr Langham."

"Pray come in and make yourself comfortable." I indicated the stands for his stick and coat. "The sideboard will support the weight of your hat and gloves." He divested himself of his outerwear with brisk, economical movements. When he was finished, I ushered him into the sitting-room and offered him his choice of armchairs. "Which would you prefer, tea or coffee?"

"Coffee, please. No milk or sugar."

I poured us a cup each, handed his to him, and sat down with mine. "I must confess my surprise that you knew my history and my concern that you knew my whereabouts."

"Let me put your mind at rest. The late Professor Moriarty maintained an intelligence network that kept him informed of all of the police force's most dangerous detectives and you were at the top of that list until your retirement. The surveillance continued until ninety-one. I had an appointment with Hamond the jewellers last year and thought I recognised you in Church Street. I made inquiries, found out where you lived, and filed the information away in case it proved useful."

I did not believe him, but he was in my house so there was little to be gained by labouring the point. "You mentioned a proposal in your letter. Before you put that proposal to me I should state that I do not feel that Mr Holmes did me a disservice – quite the contrary, I remain grateful that he prevented me from harming any other innocent people."

Moran pursed his lips and nodded slowly. "I understand. You had a reputation for ratiocination as a detective, as not only an energetic criminal agent in the field, but a scientific analyst. Let me put that to the test with a logical puzzle, the coincidence in time and space of the infallible detective and the undetected criminal. We can facilitate their temporary coexistence, but not when the criminal commits a series of murders, each of which leaves a plethora of clues, at least one of which is unplanned, and when five such crimes occur in a matter of ten weeks." He paused.

"There are two solutions: either the detective is not infallible or the criminal is not undetected – neither of which are astonishing if the coincidence to which you refer is to that of Holmes and the Whitechapel murderer in London in the latter half of eighty-eight. Personally, I favour the former solution."

"And why is that?" Moran asked, speaking very softly.

"Because I know with certainty that Holmes made a

serious error in the Baskerville murders, which were cotemporaneous with those in Whitechapel."

He raised a finger to interject. "Beryl Stapleton was the mastermind, wasn't she!"

I shook my head. "Dr Mortimer."

"Mortimer! Bravo, Mr Langham, bravo! But let me complete my argument. Holmes was consulted by Scotland Yard on receipt of the 'Dear Boss' letter, the day before the double event. He was thus almost immediately provided with two fresh crime scenes upon which to practice his science of deduction, the second almost certainly committed *ad hoc*, in addition to the previous two crimes. Six weeks later, with the Baskerville case closed – albeit erroneously – he is provided with another fresh murder to investigate yet remains unable to identify the criminal. That's incompetence, not infallibility. I think you would have solved the murders if you had still been in London and you were only ever the second most dangerous detective in the Metropolis."

"Next you will tell me that Holmes and the Whitechapel murderer are identical."

"Bravo again, Mr Langham!"

"You are making a fool of me, Colonel. I can read more likely stories in this." I picked up the *Union Jack*.

Moran leaned forward, his voice almost a whisper. "Professor Moriarty's intelligence network extended beyond the Yard to Holmes himself, including some of his disguises and three of his five boltholes. One of those boltholes was in St James's Place, off King Street. Do you know where that is?"

"Close to Mitre Square?" I guessed.

"Not even a stone's throw away."

"So Holmes killed E— S— in Dutfield's Yard, made for his bolthole in St James's Place, came across C— E— *en route*, and decided to take advantage of the circumstances to commit a second murder."

Moran nodded. "That's more like it. Now consider the description of the man seen with M— K— on the night of her death."

I remembered that a witness named G— H— had provided a detailed description of a *surly-, respectable-, and Jewish-looking* man. The suspect had, however, been of average height and Holmes was, like me, over six feet tall. Aside from this difficulty, the report had been so detailed as to be obviously either embellished or false, with the Jewish connection established by the writing on the wall in Mitre Square causing even more suspicion as to its veracity. "You are not asking me to take G— H— seriously, are you?"

"No, not that nonsense. The man that returned to the scene of the crime with M— K— earlier. Tall, stout, ginger, carrying a can of beer."

"What about him?"

Moran shook his head as if disappointed in me. "Does it not remind you of Holmes as *a drunken-looking groom, ill-kempt and side-whiskered, with an inflamed face and disreputable clothes*? Watson's words, from the Adler case. They are one and the same disguise, one and the same man."

Despite my resistance to the idea, Moran's outrageous accusation was at the very least plausible. It was less the logic and circumstance he had presented than the knowledge I already possessed of Holmes' state of mind at the time. Holmes had a breakdown in Lyon in eighty-seven, began his duel with Moriarty in the first half of eighty-eight, and had made a complete mess of the Baskerville case in the second half. In yet a further coincidence, highly suggestive albeit inconclusive, the first Whitechapel murder had been cotemporaneous with Watson meeting his first wife.

"You said you had a proposal for me?"

"I am going to visit Holmes next week to repay him

for allowing Watson to publish his account of my capture."

"I have no intention of assisting you in any action against Holmes. Not only do I remain unconvinced, but for all I know you might be the Whitechapel murderer yourself."

Moran's smile did not reach his cold, blue eyes. "I'm not going to *do* anything to Holmes. I'm simply going to tell him that I know his secret. He can spend the rest of his life brooding on that just as I have to spend the rest of mine being known by that ridiculous caricature of me in the *Strand*."

"Then what do you want me there for?"

"To stop Holmes killing me, of course."

III

Moran and I arrived at Seaford shortly after ten o'clock on Sunday morning. We emerged from the station into a bright but chill day and a brisk sea breeze. A short walk brought us to the Bay Tree Inn, where Moran had arranged the hire of a horse and trap. We set off for the tiny hamlet of Cuckmere Haven, about two miles to the east across the South Downs. Moran was no more sociable than he had been on the train, for which I was grateful, and while he drove I contemplated the circumstances of my one and only encounter with Holmes, which had occurred unnervingly close to our current location. Holmes and I had been introduced to one another at the scene of a murder under Windover Hill and it was in that same place later on the very same day that he had announced my guilt. Another quick success for the not-quite-infallible-but-definitely-not-incompetent detective. I wondered if Holmes would recognise me so many years later and, if so, if he would remember the facts of the case.

Steep white cliffs came into view as we approached a cluster of houses, but Moran kept going, continuing east up a long, green slope. We crested the rise, the wind stiff at our backs, and I could see a small estate ahead.

Moran pointed with the whip and spoke for the first time in an hour. "That's it, that's his villa."

"Does it have a name?" I asked.

"The postal address is Cuckmere Farm, but I don't know if that's the registered name. Holmes is trying to hide away from the world."

"Do you know why?"

Moran shrugged. "The same reason he retired so early."

"Which is?"

"How would I know? Maybe the pressure got to him. Maybe there wasn't enough pressure. Maybe the cracks he pasted over in eighty-eight were starting to reappear. Have you heard what he intends to do?"

"Write his *magnum opus* and keep bees."

Moran waved his whip dismissively. "He's never going to complete a textbook on detection from out here. By the time he gets the manuscript to his publisher it will be hopelessly out of date. We are in the modern age now, Langham, and the only constant is change. You cannot be modern in Cuckmere Haven."

"Very philosophical, but you're probably right, which leaves him with his bees."

"His bees." Moran smirked and I did not blame him.

The track turned away from the chalk cliffs, climbing gently, and approached the villa. The southern boundary of the estate consisted of a coppice of trees, a high brick wall overgrown with creeper plants, a low farmhouse rendered with pebbles, and a tall, thick hedge that leaned permanently to the lee. Access was provided by a green gate between the wall

and the farmhouse and I could make out a stone barn
or granary and the roof of a cottage beyond.

"Do you know how long he's been here?" I asked.

"A fortnight."

"And what staff he retains?"

"Just a housekeeper, Mrs Merrick."

Moran veered from the track, crossed the lawn in
front of the wall, and pulled up at the edge of the
coppice. He leaped down from his seat, unhitched the
horse, and applied a leather hobble. I dismounted
with less ease. The only sign of life in the villa was
smoke from one of the farmhouse chimneys, dispersed
by the wind before it could form a plume. When
Moran had finished with the horse, he jerked his head
for me to follow, and marched off through the oak,
ash, and hazel trees. Beyond the stone building was
another hedge, which had been shaped into an arch.
Moran entered and we crossed the yard at the rear of
what I now saw to be a barn. There was a garden with
an oak pergola between the house and the cottage. We
followed a paved path that led to another archway in
another hedge. Passing through this, we emerged into
an empty pasture, beyond which was the bee yard,
protected from animals by a fence and from the wind
by another tilted hedge. Erratic puffs of smoke rose
from some place out of sight and I could smell hessian,
a fuel for the smokers used to calm bees. Moran
opened the gate and entered the bee yard, which
contained six wooden hives around which hundreds –
or perhaps thousands, I had no idea – of bees flew. I
could hear the buzzing of their wings above the noise
of the breeze.

A tall, lean man in dirty white overalls, light-
coloured gloves, and a wide-brimmed beekeeper's hat
was bending down to retrieve a portable metal smoker.
Moran did not advance and neither did I. The
beekeeper picked up the smoker and turned to face us,

holding the canister at arm's length. He realised he
had company, hesitated, and set the smoker back
down. Then he strode across the yard, removing his
gloves. By the time he reached us, there were only half
a dozen bees flitting around him. He pushed both
gloves into a pocket and removed his veil and hat
carefully. The bees lost interest and flew away.

The beekeeper's hands, cheeks, nose, and ears were
covered in red and white blotches. The red blotches
were swellings, inflamed to the size of a shilling in
some cases; the white blotches were fewer, smaller,
and flatter. His nose and chin were both prominent
and the presence of a puffy, pink protuberance on each
gave him the appearance of a masculine-looking witch
from a carelessly-illustrated children's tale. The
beekeeper's gaunt visage was further distorted by a
bulge in his left cheek. Any hint of comedy was
obfuscated by the man's malignant countenance,
which communicated both fervid hatred and extreme
pain. He opened his mouth and jettisoned a long,
thick stream of brown liquid at Moran's right shoulder.
As Moran moved deftly out of the way, the beekeeper
rubbed the purple-stained fingers of his left hand into
his lower gums and coated the top of his left ear with
spittle.

"Nine —ing days. Nine —ing days is all the
retirement I am permitted."

IV

Holmes stepped between us and placed his hat upon
the gatepost. Then he retreated, removed a wet, brown
wad from his cheek and flung it at our feet. He applied
the residue of saliva and tobacco to the tip of his nose
and grimaced as his stained fingers touched the
stretched pink skin. "Thirty-two times. Thirty-two

times I have been stung and the pain is already beginning to diminish as each new stinger penetrates my flesh. The mind treats pain as the body does narcotics; tolerance is remarkably quick. The important question is, if an objective measure of pain could be established, would it share its reality with shape and number or with colour and taste..." Holmes was no longer addressing us as he wiped his fingers on his overall, adding more stains to the filthy fabric.

I was too stupefied by the shocking change in him to speak.

Moran was either less surprised or more composed, but nonetheless failed to hide his revulsion. "There's nothing worse than a man who lets himself go in middle-age."

"I have no business with two murderers that I helped to convict. If you leave now and do not return, I shall refrain from pursuing a prosecution for criminal trespass. If you do not leave, I have several weapons at my immediate disposal and I do not think that any jury will reach a verdict other than justifiable homicide when the Park Lane and Windover Hill murderers surprise me in my own home. The choice is yours."

I wondered if Holmes remembered that I had never stood trial for my crime and that Moran had been pardoned of his.

Moran replied. "You are probably correct – unless the members of that jury knew that there were a triumvirate of murderers involved: Park Lane, Windover Hill, and Whitechapel."

Holmes did not react to the accusation. Instead, he raised his left hand to indicate the direction of our retreat.

Moran waited a few seconds, turned, and opened the gate. I followed him and heard Holmes behind me. In such a fashion, we retraced our steps across the pasture, through the hedge, and across the farmyard.

Moran stepped through the second hedge and made room for me. I stood next to him so that we faced Holmes through the archway.

Moran continued. "Your East End bolthole was a few paces away from the second murder scene on the night of the double event. You murdered E— S— in Dutfield's Yard and fled for the safety of St James's Place. *En route* you happened to encounter C— E— in Mitre Square. There were no witnesses and no lights so you decided to take advantage of your good fortune. M— K—'s penultimate liaison was a tall, stout, ginger, beer-drinking cove, a description that perfectly matches your persona of Jack Griggs – or Ginger Griggs as he was better known in Whitechapel. Watson nearly gave the game away in his recounting of the Adler case, which took place a few months after the last murder, but he omitted the hair colour, which was sufficient to prevent identification. You waited for M— K— to return to her chamber in Miller's Court. When she did, you performed your experiment upon her."

Holmes reached into a pocket, withdrew a foul-smelling plug of tobacco, tucked it into his cheek, and began to grind his jaws. "Why now and why Langham?"

"By happy coincidence Mr Langham and I are North Country neighbours. As to the timing, I assume you have not read the latest *Strand*?"

"Why would – ah, I see. Watson has published the Park Lane case."

"I was happy to observe the terms of our truce. I tried to kill you and failed. You tried to hang me and failed. You remained alive, I remained free. Now I am back in the public eye, made ridiculous by the representation of Watson and Paget. Now Mr Langham will write his own Sherlock Holmes story –

perhaps he will call it 'The Adventure of the Crimson Chamber'."

Holmes smiled for the first time and a little of the tobacco juice escaped his thin lips, running down his chin to add to the stains on his overall. "Your accusation is pure slander, the evidence nothing but circumstantial."

"The necktie, said Moran, "the rifle green necktie."

Holmes' smile was replaced by a flash of unbridled savagery.

I was tired of playing the fool. "What necktie?"

"M— K—'s screaming was muffled by a necktie. The murderer left the necktie at the scene of the crime because it was so bloodied that the colour could not be discerned. The evidence was suppressed in order to assist the police in evaluating all the letters they were receiving. Ginger Griggs was never seen without his rifle green necktie."

"What difference does that make if you already have Holmes-disguised-as-Ginger-Griggs at Miller's Court?"

Moran looked at me. "The difference is that we now have the logical connection. Holmes and Ginger Griggs were one and the same. The combination of the testimony that Griggs was present at the scene of the murder and the use of his necktie in the commission of that murder establishes Griggs as the murderer. If the Whitechapel murderer was Ginger Griggs and Ginger Griggs was Holmes, then Holmes was the Whitechapel murderer."

The case against Holmes was indeed strong if he and Ginger Griggs shared their identity – which he had not denied – and situated in the context of the original puzzle of the coincidence of the infallible detective and undetected criminal. When one added the spatial coincidence of the double event and the temporal coincidence of the murders of M— A— N— and A— C—, committed in quick succession at the

time when Holmes would have realised that his
partnership with Watson would soon be terminated,
Moran's charges were all the more compelling.

Holmes addressed me. "Do whatever you think best,
Mr Langham, but bear this in mind: only four people
knew about the necktie. The inspector who was the
first to arrive at the scene of the murder, myself, the
chief inspector who was in charge of the case, and the
murderer." Then he spoke to both of us. "I remind you
that my property extends into the coppice and several
dozen yards in front of the house." His jaws laboured
once, his face reddened, and he parted his lips to
jettison more juice at us.

I turned on my heels and walked back to the trap.

V

Twenty-four hours later I turned on my heels once
more, pacing up and down my study. I had been
arrested the year before the Whitechapel murders, but
had worked with both of the detectives whom Holmes
had mentioned. Neither of them would have released
any information to either Moriarty or the press – or
anyone at all. Nor would Holmes have done so. Most
damning, I knew that my former jailer, McGinty, had
been the second policeman to arrive at the scene and
that he had no knowledge of the necktie. McGinty had
repeatedly provided me with detailed descriptions of
the appearance of the chamber in Miller's Court on the
night in question. His tedious, drunken monologues
were both excruciating and unvarying in their detail
and the facts of the first and last murder investigation
on which he had been allowed to work had been
indelibly imprinted on his brain. The necktie, had he
seen it, was precisely the sort of maudlin artefact upon
which he would have fixated. The fact that he had not

seen it lent a great deal of conviction to Holmes' claim.
And if Moran had not learned of the necktie from the
two policemen or from Holmes, then... the logic with
which he had constructed his case against Holmes
turned back on him. That logic did not necessarily
implicate Moran as the Whitechapel murderer, but it
did implicate him as knowing the identity of that
murderer either first- or second-hand. He had spoken
little on the return journey, merely begging pardon for
his claim that I was going to write about Holmes and
thanking me for my time. There had been no point in
asking him about the necktie and we had parted at
Seaford station, each making his own way home.

I continued to pace... up and down, up and down...
for over an hour.

Then I had a sudden, blinding moment of insight.
Moriarty's two main bases of operations in London
had been Hoxton and Whitechapel. If anyone in
Moriarty's organisation had known the identity of the
murderer, there was no way he would have allowed
them to continue. The horrific nature of the crimes
not only increased police activity, but led to the
establishment of various citizens' vigilance groups and
brought all sorts of unwanted attention to the area,
including plans to improve the street lighting. The
double event saw Whitechapel swarming with
constables and placed at least a temporary restriction
on criminal activities. The final murder brought even
more unwanted attention to the area and must have
proved very costly for Moriarty. Had he known who
the killer was, he would undoubtedly have set Moran
on him – unless that killer was Moran. Moran's
knowledge of the necktie established a logical
disjunction: either Moran was the killer or the killer
had told him about the necktie. Moran knew too
much – as did Holmes. But if Holmes was the killer,
how had Moran found out about the necktie? It would

be impossible because three rather than four people would have known about it: the two police officers and Holmes, who was identical with the murderer. If the murderer was Holmes, Moran could not have known about the necktie; if the murderer was known to Moran, but not Moran himself, then he would have been ordered to kill him before the necktie was used.

Another hour... up and down... up and down.

Holmes or Moran? It *had* to be Moran. Moran was a celebrated killer of man and beast and when he had tired of hunting men legally in the Army, he had turned his talents to hunting them illegally in Moriarty's pay. Holmes suspected him of killing a woman in the Scottish borders in eighty-seven; I knew there had been an assassin operating in London before that. Weren't the Whitechapel murders the sort of crimes that would be committed by someone who had tired of killing by more usual means? Holmes had spoken of tolerance to pain. Moran was precisely the sort of man who seemed to crave excitement and perhaps his tolerance to it had also grown. From the thrill of the hunt and the ecstasy of battle to the rapture of being hunted by the police – heightened by the commission of a series of ever-escalating murders. First one, then another, then two at once, and finally hours and hours spent carving up a human being beyond recognition. My only question was why he had stopped.

I decided to ask him.

I ceased my pacing and went upstairs to my bedroom. I dragged a small, steel strongbox from under my bed and unlocked it. It was here that I kept a few mementos of my former life and one which I had nowhere else to keep, McGinty's Bulldog Metropolitan Police revolver. I checked the action, bringing the hammer down on an empty cylinder. McGinty had also left seven rounds of ammunition. I loaded five. I locked the box and pushed it back under the bed. I placed the Bulldog in my pocket. Since committing murder myself, I had foresworn the use of violence, whether in the preservation of my own life or that of others. On the other hand, while I had only been a police officer for a single decade, I could not throw off the mantle of public protection as easily as Holmes. My conscience would not permit me to allow the Whitechapel murderer to remain at large. It was not a case of avenging the dead, but of protecting future victims. I must return to duty for one last case and accept whatever legal, moral, and divine consequences followed. I returned to my study for the Bradshaw.

VI

I enjoyed good fortune on the trains, changing at Darlington for Richmond and Richmond for Aysgarth. The station-master there arranged for a horse, cart, and driver to take me to West Burton. The night was dry, but cloudy and cold with very little light. My driver used a lantern to aid his passage. The entrance to the village was marked by a fork in the road that formed the north-eastern boundary of Moran's property. We continued straight ahead, down an avenue with tall trees and low stone walls on either side. After about a hundred yards, the wall to our right gave way to a hedge and the trees to a Georgian country house, a modest affair with three sash windows on either side of the doorway and two chimney stacks. There was a lamp hanging over the door, which was flanked by a pair of shrubs shaped into a screen, and the pale walls were thick with creeping ivy. We turned into the driveway, which provided barely enough space for the cart to turn, and I found myself outside the Grange at eighteen minutes to eight. I replaced my watch, checked that I could reach the Bulldog, and made use of a knocker in the shape of a lion's head.

The door was opened by a tall, slim, African woman. Her height was accentuated by the combination of a *gele* headscarf with a vertical design on her *gomesi* dress and her dark, chestnut skin was underscored by a necklace made of jet. She did not have the bearing of a servant and I was unsure how to address her. "Good evening, ma'am. My name is Roderick Langham and I have urgent business with Colonel Moran."

"I have been expecting you, Mr Langham. My name is Thandeka. Please come in and make yourself comfortable." Her English was excellent, albeit with an accent that betrayed her sub-Saharan origins.

I was disconcerted by the fact that Moran had predicted my arrival, but placed my hat, stick, gloves, and overcoat in their respective receptacles. When I had finished, Thandeka said, "Colonel Moran asked me to put you in the vestibule." She turned and I followed her graceful form.

I guessed that she was still mastering the English language because the vestibule was in fact an oak-panelled sitting-room, with four chairs arranged around a wide hearth in which a log fire crackled. The room smelled of tobacco and leather and was completely devoid of feminine influence. The four walls were covered with a hundred-odd pairs of animal horns, including two pairs of elephant tusks which were obviously from the larger African species. There was a jar of coarse-cut tobacco on the mantelpiece, nearly empty, above which was displayed the unusually large skull of a lion, its jaws distended to their utmost width. Above the jaws were a row of guns, seven in total, but with three missing. There was a single table, upon which stood an old-fashioned lamp, and I sat so as to face the door through which we had entered.

Thandeka stepped over to a cupboard in the wainscoting and said, "Would you like a drink while you wait?"

"No, thank you."

She nodded and left.

There was something very familiar about the room. I wondered if it was a replica of another I had seen or if I had read a description of it somewhere. Such musings were of little significance as I was now in the lion's den and at his mercy, with no witness to prevent him doing as he wished. I was not, as I have said, concerned for my own safety, but for that of half of the human race. In consequence, I reached into my pocket, drew the hammer of the Bulldog back, and kept a firm grip of the butt.

The house was silent aside from a clock ticking in another room.

One minute passed, then another.

I was startled to see Thandeka reappear at the door without making a sound. Her sandalled feet moved noiselessly across the wooden floor as she brought me a letter, which she offered without a word. I glanced at the doorway, depressed the hammer of the Bulldog, and took it from her outstretched hand. There were three words on the envelope: *Roderick Langham Esq.* Thandeka retraced her steps for the second time and I opened the missive.

VII

The Grange, West Burton

My dear Mr Langham – If you are reading this letter, then you have not fallen for my little deception and you will have realised that Holmes is not the Whitechapel murderer. I must admit I was misled by my intelligence, which indicated that you were both a maniac and a scribbler of unlikely stories – a combination I could not resist unleashing upon Holmes in retaliation for Watson's libellous sketch. Having met Holmes in his declining years, however, I think he is doing more damage to his own reputation than I could ever have achieved myself. I hope you will forgive both my attempt at deception and the impersonal nature of this communication.

I have been commissioned to hunt a dragon in the Welsh Marches, an expedition which will either prove to be the summit of my career or an ignominious hoax. Whichever the case, I may be gone for some time. By way of reparation on my part, you may be interested to learn that Professor Moriarty was the Whitechapel murderer. He claimed he was making a scientific study of pain, for which he had invented a new unit, the dol. *It was nonsense, of course, and after what he did in that woman's chamber I told him I would resign before he brought destruction on all of us. There were no more experiments in that particular branch of science.*

Yours sincerely

Sebastian R. Moran
October 12th 1903

7. The Devil's Hollow

...There entered in at the east window of the church a dark unproportioned thing about the bigness of a football, and went along the wall on the pulpit side; and suddenly it seemed to break with no less sound than if a hundred cannons had been discharged at once; and therewithal came a most violent storm and tempest of lightning and thunder as if the church had been full of fire...

The Wrath of God
Reverend Fr. Austen, 1868

I

Shortly after the coronation of the great uncle of Europe, I took to frequenting the public bar of the Royal Hotel every Wednesday evening. The change of my routine was not motivated by a desire to acknowledge the passing of the austere era that had exhausted first my youth and then my good health, but to give my housekeeper, the aptly-named Mrs Knaggs, a night off during the week. For some reason I could not fathom, she had no objection to leaving me to my own devices on Saturday and Sunday evenings, but would under no circumstances attend her midweek bridge club if I was in residence. Being a naturally reclusive individual, I was initially concerned that my presence in the hotel would be misconstrued as a desire for company, but in four years I had only

been approached on three occasions, exclusively by
members of the Whitby Literary and Philosophical
Society, the only society of which I was a member. In
order to discourage company, I would arrive at the
hotel at half-past six with a pile of newspapers, two to
three copies each of *The Yorkshire Post*, the *Daily Mail*,
The Morning Post, *The New York Times*, and the
Boston Herald. I would take a table in the most
secluded corner, next to the sash window overlooking
the lower harbour, the East Cliff, and the ruins of
Whitby Abbey. I would order a pot of coffee, light up
my pipe, and study the periodicals until ten o'clock, by
which time I could return home free from guilt. On
most weeks the editor of the local *Dailygraph*, a
flamboyant American by the name of Largo Delapena,
entertained his colleagues, friends, and the curious at
the next table but one, throwing a veil of chatter,
clinking glasses, smoke, and good cheer across my
sanctuary.

On the night in question, Delapena had arrived
shortly after me, wished me good evening – for he was
always immaculate in his manners – and indulged
himself and his half-dozen associates in a manner of
which our cheerful but somewhat dissolute monarch
would have approved. Nothing extraordinary occurred
until a couple of hours later, when a pale man of about
forty years of age entered the bar-room, demanded a
bottle of brandy from the steward, and sat down at the
table across the sash window from me. He filled his
glass to the brim, drank it down in one swift draught,
refilled the glass, and lit a cigarette. While this may
have been *de rigeur* for saloons in the American West
or the Australian Outback, it was unusual behaviour
for a gentleman in a luxury hotel at a seaside resort in
Yorkshire. What's more, he certainly maintained the
appearance of a gentleman, being a dapper little man
in a smart black suit with cigarettes from Sobranie of

London. I had no wish to intrude, however, so I reapplied myself to the trans-Atlantic news from Boston.

Three-quarters of an hour later, I happened to look up from a review of Mr Parry's *The Scarlet Empire* and noticed a cloud of smoke hovering above the alcoholic gentleman. He had already consumed half of his bottle of Armagnac, filled his ash-receiver, and was drawing heavily on a Black Russian. I studied him surreptitiously, from the corner of my eye, as I refilled my pipe. He was, as I had initially discerned, small of small stature, wan of complexion, and four decades old. He had pitch black hair and a generous but neatly-trimmed beard, although neither had felt the touch of a brush recently. His beard was slightly discoloured beneath his mouth, perhaps the beginning of a grey streak. His suit was complemented with a necktie, embroidered silk waistcoat, and impeccably-shined boots. From the absence of a hat, stick, and overcoat – and the readiness with which the steward had acquiesced to his demand – I deduced that he was a guest of the hotel. Much of his face was concealed by the beard, which made his pallor seem even more deathly than it really was. He was staring directly ahead, which should have brought me under his scrutiny, but his gaze was blank, eyes unfocused. I noticed that he was sweating and that his hand shook as he raised the cigarette to his lips. The perspiration and palpitation could have been either the cause or the effect of his alcohol consumption.

I finished packing my pipe, but did not light it, choosing instead to continue my clandestine surveillance of the gentleman over the top of the *Boston Herald*.

He smoked his Black Russian down to the gold filter, stubbed it out in the ash-receiver, and opened his cigarette case. It was empty. He cursed, retrieved a wooden box from his coat pocket, and removed a handful of cigarettes. He lit another cigarette with a permanent match and started filling the case. He stopped a few seconds later, before the case was full, smiled to himself, and laughed rather loudly for someone sitting on his own. When he had smoked his cigarette down to the filter, he dropped it in the ash-receiver, and poured more Armagnac from the bottle. He stopped when the glass was one third full and consumed the contents before he had returned the bottle to the table. Then he rose, withdrew a money-wallet from his coat, fumbled inside it, and stepped over to the bar. He threw a five pound note on the counter – more than ten times his bill – and marched out towards reception. The steward's mouth dropped open. He looked at me and I waved for him to keep the money. I slipped my pipe into my pocket, donned my hat, picked up my stick, and left my overcoat behind.

I arrived in the reception hall in time to see the gentleman walk out the main entrance. I went after him. It was nearly ten o'clock and few people had braved the cold, wet night. He had turned left and was now striding along East Terrace towards the cliff. I followed, bending forward against the stiff sea breeze blowing drizzle in my face. The gentleman left the road, passed the footpath leading down to the pier, and continued for the cliff, high above the bathing beach. I am, as my name suggests, unusually tall, so I was able to close the distance between us without exerting any more effort than my quarry.

I was some twenty feet away when he slowed down to a halt a short distance from the cliff-edge.

I picked up my pace.

He reached inside his right trouser pocket.

I had not committed an act of violence in over

nineteen years, but the movements came easily, without conscious thought.

His hand emerged clutching a Derringer. He raised it to his right temple. He drew the hammer back.

I hacked at the pistol with my Penang-lawyer, knocking the weapon into the air and over the cliff.

He turned around, dazed and uncertain, seeing me for the first time. He swayed slightly, unsteady on his feet.

"Who... who are you?"

"My name is Roderick Langham."

He blinked and lost focus again. "I'm Wilfrid Fletcher. I'm... I *was* the Chief Magistrate of the Pitcairn Islands. I have seen terrible things... monsters."

"So have I," I replied.

He nodded slowly.

"I think you had better come along with me. I live just a little way down this road."

II

I ensconced Fletcher in my study at No.10 Flowergate rather than the larger room below that served as my sitting-room, dining-room, and library. My reasons were twofold: I did not want Mrs Knaggs disturbing us, which she would if she saw the lights on downstairs, and I was worried Fletcher would disappear if he was too close to the front door. My kitchen is, inexplicably, on the first floor of the house, and I was able to keep an eye on him while I prepared refreshment for us. I decided that we had both had too much stimulation for one evening, so I brewed a pot of tea and toasted the last of the day's bread. I needn't have fretted for Fletcher. He followed me meekly and, after making use of the water-closet, collapsed in the armchair. I lit the fire while the tea leaves were drawing and the toast cooking. When I returned with a tray, he had not stirred. I placed a cup of tea and two rounds of buttered toast on the side-table next to him, set the tray on my desk, and drew the dining chair closer.

"I noticed there were only three chairs at the table downstairs," said Fletcher, as I took my first drink of tea.

"Yes, I spend long hours at my desk and find the support eases my back pain."

"You are a writer?"

"Of a sort, yes. I have been a soldier, a detective, and an invalid. Now I write mystery and adventure stories for magazines." His attention seemed to drift away. "Perhaps you would be kind enough to tell me of the circumstances that have brought you to this pass?" He nodded. "May I ask you to be entirely frank? You said you have seen monsters. I saw one long ago in a place called Assam, near the Himalayas. I saw another, more recently and much closer, for this, also, has been one of the dark places of the earth. You need not fear my disdain or derision."

"Perhaps I should fortify myself first." I waited while Fletcher ate a slice of toast. When he was finished, he had a long drink of tea, sighed, and began. "My people are the Fletchers of Yeadon, near Leeds, and we are a cursed race. I am grateful that the curse runs only in the male line of the family. I have had six brothers and five sisters. All of my sisters are married with issue of their own. The dilution of their blood with that of their husbands seems to have lifted the curse, for between them they have fourteen offspring, seven boys and seven girls. Neither I nor my brothers have offspring. Two of us have reached thirty, but personal and professional success remained elusive. My eldest brother, Edward, served the 5th Northumberland

Fusiliers with distinction in the Black Mountain Expedition, but had only reached the rank of major when he was killed in action in South Africa. I am thirty-one years of age, have been a colonial administrator ever since leaving school, but never rose beyond the rank of assistant commissioner. I spent the last four years in the Pitcairn Islands. I doubt you have even heard of them."

I was dismayed to learn that Fletcher was in fact more than twenty years my junior. "I believe they are in the very middle of the great Pacific Ocean."

"Indeed. There are four islands, but only one is inhabited and that with less than one hundred souls. The nearest land is over one hundred leagues away and barely less remote. They are quite literally the backwater of the British Empire, populated almost entirely by blood relations, and plagued by the biological and social problems that accompany hyperbolic homogeneity. I have been Chief Magistrate since the annexation, with little prospect of promotion to commissioner or lieutenant governor. I am now the only one of my brothers living and were it not for your gracious intervention, would have completed the curse's work on my own." He paused to take more tea.

"That seems remarkable. May I ask how the others died?"

"Lancelot was my parent's third child and died shortly after his birth. Our family was free from tragedy for twenty-six years, but then I lost three brothers in less than twelve months. Harold was listed as missing in action during the Matabele War, Arthur was a victim of death by misadventure in the Pyrenees, and Herbert died in strange circumstances not too far from here, near Kingston upon Hull. Edward's death left only myself and my youngest brother, Henry. He went into the priesthood, but was – like the rest of us – unsuccessful in his vocation. He was twenty-nine before he assumed the responsibilities of a vicar and then in a parish so remote to have been equivalent to my lowly dominion. Are you familiar with Great Billington?"

"No, I am not."

"It is a tiny hamlet on the moors, a few miles from Goathland." I knew the moors very well and had visited Goathland several times so I was surprised by this intelligence. "Henry took up residence at the vicarage in the summer and it was with great sadness but not great surprise that I was informed of his death last month. I resigned my office immediately and begged passage on the naval vessel that brought me the news. I returned post-haste, ahead of my luggage, arriving in Whitby last Thursday."

"May I ask a question?"

"Certainly." Fletcher made use of the opportunity to take the second slice of toast.

"I applaud your filial love, but that seems a drastic step to take. Would your superiors in the colonial service not have afforded you a leave of absence?"

Fletcher wiped his mouth with his handkerchief. "I was about to throw in the towel anyway, but I'll come back to that later if you like. On Friday, I met with Reverend Perkins, Henry's superior in the church, and Doctor Abbott, who had performed the post-mortem examination. Henry had been laid to rest in the Church of Saint Mary by Perkins in the interim. Curiously, he had registered my name alone as his next of kin. Indeed, now that I think on it, I believe my sisters are unaware that they are down to their last brother. Abbott informed me that Henry had died from a lightning strike. I was told the poor chap's exterior was covered in what doctors call 'feathering', a fern-pattern made by broken blood vessels; his interior was far worse, with his intestines burned beyond recognition and both eardrums burst. Abbott said he would have died instantly, but I am not sure if I believe him.

"Now you might think that given the curse to which I believe the male Fletchers are subject, a lighting strike is precisely the sort of nemesis I or my brother should expect. You would no doubt be correct, but there were two points that piqued my curiosity. First, in the only letter from Henry that reached me prior to news of his death, he mentioned several pagan practices in the village. He said that although the population ostensibly venerated Saint Cuthbert, they actually belonged to a religious cult known as the Old Faith and worshipped a pre-Christian deity of unknown origin. Second, I thought it strange that a hamlet boasted a vicar. I'm no expert in church hierarchy, but Great Billington has a population of forty-odd souls and should have been allocated a deacon rather than a priest. It seemed somewhat like giving the Pitcairn Islands its own governor. I mentioned this to Perkins, but he said that the village had been bigger in medieval times and that the post was traditional, in much the way that Whitby retains its own bishop. After visiting Henry's grave, I didn't have anything with which to occupy my time, so I found the Literary and Philosophical Society and asked to look at the local records. I couldn't find any mention of Great Billington, which made me think Perkins' story a fabrication."

"I have a County Series map of the North Riding. Would you mind if I fetched it? Thank you. Do polish off the rest of the toast if you're hungry."

When I returned Fletcher was doing just that. I located Goathland on the map. With Fletcher's assistance, I found Great Billington in a natural depression between Danby High Moor and Wheeldale Moor, under Pike Hill Moss. I resumed my seat as Fletcher resumed his tale.

"I went back to Perkins, told him I was going to visit Great Billington, and asked if I might stay in the vicarage, assuming that the hamlet had no hostelry. He did everything in his power to stop me bar refusing to give me the key, but I did not relent. I took the train to Goathland on Saturday morning. The inn-keeper there also attempted to dissuade me from going to Great Billington. It was only when I told him that I would walk if he did not provide me with transport that he hired me a horse and cart at an extortionate price. He also pressed a curious little star-shaped stone on me, which he said I should keep upon my person at all times. I reached the village quickly and found the vicarage without any trouble. Within the hour, I received an invitation to luncheon with the squiress at Billington Manor, an elderly widow by the name of Potter. She too was full of the superstitions of the area and told me how the isolation of the community had contributed to the continuation of certain ancient traditions. I must admit that I had already seen disturbing signs of the insularity with which I was familiar from my colonial experience." Fletcher shuddered. "Mrs Potter practically begged me to stay at the manor and, when I wouldn't, warned me to remain indoors if there was a storm.

"The next day was Sunday and I wondered if there would be a service in the absence of any official representative of the church. And this is where things really become strange. Individually or in pairs, every single person in the village except Mrs Potter performed a small ceremony in the churchyard, laying some offering before a little statue. The ritual was perfectly coordinated such that no person, couple, or family met any other. I watched the whole thing from the vicarage window. I returned to Billington Manor to ask Mrs Potter about it and she told me of the Old Faith and showed me an old book that catalogued the practice. Despite the fact that she'd been harping on about pagans and druids, the title concerned New England, not old England, so I confess I didn't pay much attention."

"Was it *Of Evill Sorceries done in New-England of Daemons in no Humane Shape*?" I asked.

"Yes, I think that was it. Why?"

"Remarkable, quite remarkable. I shall let you finish."

"I was intending to return to Goathland the following day, none the wiser and disappointed that my brother's last months had been spent in such a wretched place, but the barometer fell rapidly on Monday morning. I decided to stay and see the phenomenon that had put paid to poor Henry. At midday, with the clouds brooding overhead and the atmosphere tense, the villagers began to gather in the churchyard. They started chanting in an alien tongue and were swaying in unison as if under hypnosis by the time I arrived. I tried to engage several of them in conversation, but none took any notice. When I reached the front of the crowd, I was astonished to find Mrs Potter. I tried to talk to her, but she took no notice either so I picked up the statuette." Fletcher shuddered again, more violently this time. "Suddenly, the chanting stopped and the squiress pointed at me, letting forth an awful high-pitched screech. Something like *he has violated Cath-arta*. Then... my God... then the entire village – about forty men, women, and children – tried to tear me limb from limb."

"How did you escape?"

"When they threw me to the ground, the stone the inn-keeper had given me fell out and they backed away as if it was an incendiary device. I fled the churchyard for Billington Manor, stole a horse, and rode back to Goathland. I am not a great rider, but had some small practice in the Pitcairn Islands. My arrival in Goathland was contemporaneous with the train – on which I leaped without ceremony. I'm afraid that I spent the rest of Monday and most of Tuesday drinking. I won the Derringer off a Moldavian sailor in a game of Old Maid last night and decided to use it this evening. I've not thanked you for saving my life yet, but the thing is, I'm not sure if I wouldn't be better off dead. I hope you understand."

"Your life is your own; you may do with it what you wish. I do hope, however, that you will at least postpone a final decision until you have had a good night's rest." He nodded. "It is such a pity that you lost the stone in the struggle; I should like to have seen it."

"I didn't. I picked it up before I shot off. I thought it might be useful if I was caught."

"You have displayed a remarkable presence of mind, Mr Fletcher, and I suspect there is nothing wrong with your nerves that a few weeks' rest won't cure. May I?"

He dropped a small, green rock in the palm of my hand. The material was soapstone and it had been carved with very little skill, producing a warped five-pointed star. There was an engraving in the centre, which also evinced poor workmanship and vaguely resembled a flaming eye. I had read several descriptions of the star-stone before, though I had not thought that I would ever see one. I realised why the device in the centre had been described as both a flaming eye and a flaming pillar, but assuming that I was holding the genuine article, it was a flaming eye.

"Do you know what it is?" asked Fletcher.

"Yes, it is called an Elder Sign and I think you had better occupy my guest bedroom tonight."

III

I rose earlier than usual on Thursday morning, roused Mrs Knaggs, and proceeded to visit first the Royal Hotel, then the bathing beach, and finally the police station. I woke Fletcher at nine o'clock and broke my habit of having a light breakfast to join him for a hearty – and meaty – offering from Mrs Knaggs. The clock had just struck ten when we left the table for the comfort of the armchairs in front of the fire. I prepared my after-breakfast pipe to accompany my coffee and offered Fletcher a cigar, but he declined, claiming that he had consumed too much alcohol and tobacco in the last three days.

"I have a proposal to put to you, Mr Fletcher, if I may. Allow me to begin by recounting my movements this morning. I went back to the hotel first-thing and asked who you were and if anyone had seen you depart last night. When the attendant said not, I mentioned that I had seen you at the cliff edge when I left and that I was concerned for your safety – I shall explain in a moment. At dawn, I began searching the beach for your Derringer. I was able to make a relatively accurate prediction as to where it landed given the angle and force of my blow and the trajectory of the firearm's descent. I am so glad that your hand is less swollen, by the way. After an hour I was convinced that the pistol had been swept out to sea by the tide. I then visited the police station, where I told the constable a version of the evening's events. I said that I was concerned for your safety and felt responsible for not having approached you when I saw you atop the cliff. I made no suggestion of suicide, only that you may have been unsteady on your feet due to the amount of alcohol you had consumed. It is far too early for the police to investigate, but the constable made a note in the occurrence book."

I lit my pipe before continuing. "I have long suspected that North-East Yorkshire is as much, if not more, of a centre for the worship of the Old Ones as the notorious Miskatonic Valley in New England. This is, I believe, the Old Faith to which your brother referred and is quite simply the cult of elemental evil. There are four Old Ones – demons, devils, or elementals – one each for the elements that the ancients believed constituted the basic building blocks of the universe. Thus far, I have discovered three sites, at which all signs of worship have been destroyed. The earth temple is at Towton, the scene of the bloodiest battle ever to have been fought on Britain's soil. The air temple is at a place called Faxfleet, at the confluence of the Humber and the Trent, and used to be a Templar Preceptory. The water temple is in Scarborough, underneath the castle. From various cross-references I was able to make, I guessed that the fire temple was somewhere on the North York Moors. It seems you have found it for me and that, unlike the others, the cult of *Cthuga* is alive and well."

Fletcher nodded, but the strain on his face was terrible to see. "That was the name Mrs Potter screamed."

"The book she showed you is a history of both the elementals themselves and their respective cults and contains all the details of the rites required for the revival of the Old Faith. It is known as the *New Dunnich Manuscript* and was written by an anonymous high priest of the cult, believed to have emigrated to the New World in the seventeenth or eighteenth century. The manuscript seems either to have either made its way back to here or to have been copied prior to the high priest's departure. Now, do you not think it extraordinary that you just happened to find yourself a hotel frequented by the only man in England with this knowledge?"

"I must confess, Mr Langham, that nothing would surprise me at this juncture."

I removed the Elder Sign from my pocket. "This is a symbol of the Elder Gods, a quartet who are said to struggle with the elementals for the soul of mankind. The gods are known by the names of the races that settled on the east coast – the Celts, Romans, Saxons, and Vikings – as Nodens, Mercury, Donar, and Tir. Over the last two millennia, their worshippers, forming a kind of counter-cult, have destroyed three of the four temples of the Old Ones. The earth temple at Towton and the air temple at Faxfleet were both razed above and below ground. A grove of trees was planted on the site at Towton and is now a small wood, although it is the only wood I have ever known devoid of all fauna. The Templars built their preceptory on the ashes of the air temple. Now, not even the foundations of the preceptory are visible to the casual visitor. The water temple at Scarborough was sealed by worshippers of Nodens, but not destroyed. It now lies directly under the chapel in Scarborough Castle. I suspect that your unfortunate brother's church has either been built on the site of the fire temple or is a disguised fire temple. It is not unknown for the worshippers of elemental evil to conceal their cult under the trappings of Christianity in much the same way as the cult of the Elder Gods. I think you should keep this." I handed Fletcher the Elder Sign. "It has been given to you for a purpose and it is not mine to take."

He shrugged and accepted the stone. "Do you believe all this – in the Elder Gods and the Old Ones?"

I puffed on my pipe. "I believe that cult and counter-cult have battled each other in secrecy over the centuries. I believe that the counter-cult is extinct, as are the earth, air, and water cults. I had hoped that the fire cult had also been consigned to history, but your tale indicates otherwise. I do not know if there is anything behind the cults. Though I am sceptical by nature and scientific by training, I have seen evidence of more than my education and experience can explain. The status of the water temple as sealed rather than destroyed may, for example, explain the profusion of giant sea creatures whose skeletons have been found on these shores. The hypothesis that the rock is particularly well-suited to preserving fossils accounts for the fact that the vast majority of the remains are prehistoric. The hypothesis that the priests of Dagon summoned his servants accounts for the fact that a small minority of the remains are more recent. I do not know which is correct – perhaps they are both true."

The blood drained from Fletcher's face. "I have seen such a creature. In July. I used to join the crayfishermen when they set their nets and rigged their moorings in Bounty Bay. On this day, a shark surfaced alongside. One of the men sounded the alarm; luckily none were in the water. I made some study of sharks during my time in the Pacific and I am able to calculate their length with precision, using the distance between their dorsal and caudal fins. This shark was as long as the pier itself."

"And how long was that?"

"One hundred and fifteen feet."

I put my proposal to him.

IV

Telegram from Roderick Langham Esq. of No.10 Flowergate, Whitby to Mrs W.H. Potter, Billington Manor, Great Billington:

Whitby GPO, 11.16 am, December 13, 1906:
WOULD LIKE TO DISCUSS ACCESS TO NEW
ENGLAND MANUSCRIPT IN YOUR
POSSESSION IN EXCHANGE FOR ACCESS TO
LETTERS OF REVEREND DYER IN MINE STOP
WILL CALL AT MIDDAY ON SATURDAY STOP
LANGHAM

Agony Column, *Dailygraph*, Thursday December 13th
1906:

Missing – Mr Wilfrid Fletcher, formerly of
Yeadon, Leeds and Adamstwon, Pitcairn Islands
and presently a guest at the Royal Hotel. Last
seen on East Terrace at approximately 10pm last
night. Mr Roderick Langham, of No.10
Flowergate, fears that some harm may have come
to him, and will pay three guineas to anyone who
can provide information as to his whereabouts.

V

I set off for Great Billington in my wagonette at a few
minutes before nine on Saturday morning. I left an
anxious Fletcher smoking one Black Russian after the
next in our shared sitting-room at Mallyan Spout
Hotel. As a precaution, I had employed a skill I had
not had cause to use for many years and disguised him
by dying his hair and beard and applying greasepaint
to his skin. The devices narrowed the gap between us
completely with the result that Fletcher was not out of
place among the other elderly ladies and gentlemen
who had come to Goathland to take the waters. As a
further precaution, he had adopted the alias of
Williams and retired immediately to our suite, where
he had remained ever since. The morning was cold
with an icy breeze blowing from the west, where dark

clouds brooded in a bruised sky. Although Great
Billington was less than four miles hence, I was
concerned about losing my way, for the hamlet was
accessible only by a series of the faintest of trails, made
by the infrequent wheels of the grocer's wagon. There
was no postal delivery to Great Billington and what
little post arrived waited at Goathland General Post
Office until the grocer sent his delivery or one of Mrs
Potter's servants made a rare appearance.

I left the village by the Egton Road, with Scar Wood
and the River Esk on my right, and gently rolling
moorland all around. When the road turned north, I
continued west along a stony track which cut through
the wood, crossed the river on a rickety old bridge, and
passed the entrance to a prosperous-looking farm
before curving south. It was a relief to turn out of the
wind, but I kept my scarf wrapped around my face and
my hat pulled low on my ears. I could see a small grove
of trees a few hundred yards ahead, which I was
expecting from committing my map to memory. I was
progressing as planned.

Fletcher and I had arrived in Goathland the
previous day. While he kept out of sight, I continued
to pursue the inquiries initiated on Thursday. From
the inn-keeper at The Lancaster Arms, a man by the
name of Talbot whom I had met on a previous visit, I
had discovered that the Elder Sign he had pressed
upon Fletcher was the property of an American
gentleman by the name of Keane. Two years ago, he
had set out on precisely the same journey as Fletcher
and failed to return. The stone had fallen out of his
pocket when he had mounted his cart, but Talbot had
only discovered it after his departure. Keane had never
been seen again, nor had Talbot's cart, which was why
he had charged Fletcher an extortionate price, and
required me to buy both wagonette and horse
(although he did offer to buy them back at a slightly

reduced price in the unlikely event that I returned). When I asked him what the danger was in Great Billington, he said "witches" and refused to elaborate. Following Keane's disappearance, the police had made inquiries in the hamlet to no avail and Talbot had sent a letter to his address in Arkham, Massachusetts which was returned to sender. I was the first person to ask about him – albeit indirectly – and he was the first person to have visited Great Billington since Talbot had acquired ownership of the inn at the turn of the century.

The track turned west again and the land began to sink. The green fields of the farms gave way to patches of purple heather that meandered under barren brown hills. Egton High Moor rose steeply to the north and Wheeldale Moor more gently to the south, both white with snow. After a couple of hundred yards, I fell in alongside Wheeldale Gill, passing Scar End Wood at the foot of Wheeldale Moor. As I descended, the wind speed dropped and the first snowflakes began to fall, dusting the landscape.

My second inquiry had been at the post office, where the postmaster confirmed that one of his employees had delivered the telegram to Mrs Potter's butler, a Mr Whateley, in person. There had been no reply, from which I assumed that Mrs Potter was desirous of our meeting – either lured by my mention of *The Letters of Reverend Dyer* or concerned about Fletcher revealing her conspiracy to authorities religious or civil. I had met with both Dr Abbott and Reverend Perkins on Thursday. I knew Dr Abbott quite well, for he was my own physician, and he had confirmed Reverend Fletcher's death by lightning. I had then visited Reverend Perkins on the pretext of concern about Fletcher, whom I had already reported to the police as missing. Perkins confirmed that Fletcher had come to see him, but did not give the

impression that there was anything sinister about
Great Billington and did not try to dissuade me when I
mentioned I was going to look for Fletcher there.

The track curled around Pike Hill, the only high
ground in the hollow I had entered. Ahead, I could see
the white slopes of Rosedale Moor. Great Billington
was somewhere off to my left, through the trees of
Pike Hill Moss. I spotted a small stone bridge between
the boughs, the only evidence of human habitation
beyond. On the other side, gravel had been strewn in
imitation of a track. The wood or "moss" was narrow
and the gravel became firmer as I emerged onto a
particularly barren stretch of low moor. It did not take
much imagination to call Shakespeare's blasted heath
– with all its connotations – to mind and the
coincidence of a heavier snowfall was not reassuring.
The path descended again, winding off to the right. As
I rounded the bend, I saw two small cottages, one on
either side of the path, a few dozen yards apart. The
path curved left, falling off further, and I shortly
arrived at the hub of the hamlet, half a dozen cottages
dotted around a junction shaped like a "T". There were
no people or even animals to be seen. The only sign of
life was smoke from two of the chimneys. Fletcher had
provided me with a detailed description of Great
Billington so I knew that Billington Manor was to the
left, out of sight behind a screen of pine trees, and the
church and vicarage off to the right, barely visible
behind the snowflakes being blown in my face. I had
made good time – it was a little after ten – so I turned
right.

The church and vicarage sat opposite each other
about a hundred yards up the path. There was one
other house on this side of the settlement and it
looked just as empty as the vicarage. The vicarage was
a Tudor cottage in better repair than any of the houses
I had seen thus far. The church was much older and

may even have been Norman if the arched top and heavy oaken door of the vestibule were original features. I brought the wagonette to a halt, dismounted, and threw a blanket over the horse. I opened the gate and entered the churchyard. It was filled with tombstones, most of which were broken or cracked, and some of which bore inscriptions that were still legible – at least in part. *Jabez Jonathan Dunlock and Elizabeth ... Gone to The Lord, AD 1687 ... Eleanor Anne Allen ... Passed Away AD 1701 ... Robert Francis Whateley, Who died ... aged 44 years*. There were a large number of Dunlocks and Whateleys and Allens laid to rest, but no Potters. I wondered if the late squire had his own mausoleum and saw a small but substantially-built structure at the side of the church. I walked over, my shoes crunching through the settling snow. The stonework was indeed a tomb, with two bones carved at right angles and surmounted by a skull in lieu of the usual cross over the door. A macabre conceit typical of the sixteenth and seventeenth centuries. The emblem was weathered and difficult to discern courtesy of defacing by means of a chisel or similar instrument. There was no family name on the mausoleum. I left the resting place of the Potters – if that's what it was – and continued through the graveyard, finding more Dunlocks and Whateleys, as well as a few Perkinses, before reaching a lych-gate. I opened the gate and entered the portico.

The small stone carving Fletcher had described was resting on a ledge where it was only visible from outside the graveyard. It was about nine inches in diameter, roughly circular in shape, and made of an unfamiliar brown granite. What looked like spikes protruded from all sides of the globe, which balanced on four particularly sturdy specimens. On closer inspection, the spikes resembled tentacles or flames. Given what I already knew, I guessed that the idol was a very crude representation of a ball of fire. If my researches had been accurate, Cthuga was served by ball lightning in the same way that Dagon was served by sea monsters past and present. Famously, a ball of lightning had entered the Church of St Hilda in Whitby during the consecration ceremony in 1867. Several people were injured and one killed, which had prompted much speculation on the wrath of God and the desirability of having a Catholic church in the town. I speculated as to how Fletcher had picked the idol up. It must be heavy and there were no spaces large enough for a firm grip between the flames. I leaned my stick against the gate and rubbed my gloved hands together while I considered where to place them.

As I reached for the idol, I heard the crunch of footsteps in the graveyard. I quickly retrieved my stick and turned to the gate in time to see a small, solid figure emerge through the falling snow. The man stopped behind the gate and stared at me. He was about five and a quarter feet in height, thickly-set, and of an indeterminate age between twenty-five and fifty. The face under the bowler hat was hideously ugly. The man had a large, bulbous nose, a protruding lower lip, and his eyes – which were set very close together – were not quite symmetrical. His skin was an unnatural colour, with a very light purplish tint, and he appeared to have failed to shave the left side of his face as closely as the right. Never before had I seen so many signs of consanguineous breeding in a single individual. I doubted whether Fletcher had seen worse on the Pitcairn Islands. The man opened the gate.

"Good day," I said.

"Mr Langham?" he asked. "My name is Whateley. I'm the butler at Billington Manor. Mrs Potter will see you now."

I took out my watch. It was not yet eleven. "Our appointment is for midday."

"I will drive you there in your cart."

I waited a few seconds, but saw no reason to prolong the standoff. I walked through the gate, towering over Whateley as I passed, and retraced my steps. Thick clouds eclipsed the sun as swathes of snow descended to earth.

VI

I saw very little of the hamlet or the manor during the short journey. Though the wind was at our backs, visibility was reduced to twenty yards or so. The manor was protected from prying eyes by a line of pine trees. Once we had penetrated these, I could only see a lawn on either side – now a flat white blanket – and then what appeared to be a modest stone mansion of two storeys, with a turret above the vehicular entrance. We drove past this to the main entrance, which faced south. The walls of the manor were already white, the snow clinging to the ubiquitous ivy. Whateley stopped the wagonette and I dismounted. The moment my left foot touched the ground, the snowfall stopped. It was quite disconcerting and I glanced up, but the heavy black clouds had not moved. The front door opened before I reached it. I could not suppress a start when I saw who stood behind it. She could have been Whateley's twin and I couldn't help wonder whether she was his sister, mother, daughter, wife, or some combination of these. Fletcher must have found himself right back in his worst Pacific nightmare. *This, also, is one of the dark places of the earth*. The female Whateley took my hat, stick, scarf, and overcoat without a word. The reception area was a room rather than a hall. It was appointed in a practical manner little given to decoration, with cocoanut matting on the floor and stairs and light-coloured oak panelling on the walls. There were no paintings or mirrors.

"Mrs Potter will see you in the library."

My diminutive companion led me through a similarly plain parlour into a long, narrow room with bookshelves covering three of the four walls. The remaining wall boasted four sash windows, with a settee and roll-top writing desk positioned so as to benefit from the natural light – though there was not much of it at present. Scattered around the rest of the room were a tall gas lamp, a large globe, and a lectern supporting a medieval illustrated manuscript. Above the back panel of the desk, a white bonnet bobbed up and down. My escort grunted, a face appeared beneath the cap, and Mrs Potter stopped her writing. She dismissed her servant and rose.

I was relieved to see that she bore no resemblance whatsoever to the Whateleys. She was, in fact, remarkably tall for a woman and in remarkably vigorous health for a sexagenarian. She stood straight-backed and steady, her movements were clean and brisk. She had an aristocratic, aquiline profile and a skin tanned by the sun but without excessive wrinkling. I imagined her leading an active, outdoor lifestyle, and could only conjecture as to what kept her in this godforsaken place. When Mrs Potter stood before me, I realised she was in mourning. The white bonnet was a widow's cap and she was clothed in the bombasine and crepe of the recently-bereaved. Our late queen had made prolonged mourning fashionable, however, so there was no way of telling when Mr Potter had died.

"Mr Langham, I am Mrs Potter." I heard the sound of thunder in the distance.

"How do you do?"

She did not answer, but indicated the settee and

resumed her chair, adjusting it so that she was facing me instead of her letters.

"Allow me to thank you for receiving me on such short notice, madam. I— "

"May I come directly to the point, Mr Langham?"

"Of course."

"I have consented to this intrusion because I should like to know how the contents of my library have become the subject of gossip in Whitby. I can only imagine that it is the doing of Mr Fletcher, the brother of our late vicar. Is that correct?"

"Yes." I did not volunteer any further information.

"Mr Fletcher arrived last week, obviously in a state of distress. I received him for luncheon that day and tea for the next. He spent the interval asking the villagers pointless and accusatory questions, as if they had been responsible for calling down the lightning that killed the vicar. My impression on his second visit was that he was mentally unhinged. This was confirmed when he burst into the church and disrupted my service."

"You were leading a church service?" I asked.

Thunder rumbled in the distance, nearer than before. "Yes. In the absence of a clergyman, the locals look to me for spiritual leadership and I have taken on the responsibilities of a sort of lay-deacon from time to time. Great Billington is not popular with vicars, who tend to move on to less remote parishes as soon as decency permits. My late husband and I valued this very remoteness above all else and chose to remain in the place of his ancestors in order to pursue our collection of hermetic and arcane manuscripts in private. You will notice a large number of antiquarian tomes on these shelves, many are rare and some unique. What I am least desirous of is for the contents of my library to become public knowledge. It would bring no end of... *visitors*." Her expression made it clear that I was the first of these undesirables. "Do you disagree that I have the right to privacy, Mr Langham?"

"No madam, I do not, but I hope that you have included a provision for the collection in your legacy."

She ignored my comment and continued. "Thank you. I beg you to ask Mr Fletcher to respect my privacy."

"I'm afraid I am unable to do that. Mr Fletcher has disappeared and I fear that he may have come to some harm. I was, as far as I know, the last to see him. He was very maudlin and heavily under the influence of alcohol. When we parted, I saw him walk towards the West Cliff. He has not been seen since and I confess I feel responsible for leaving him."

"There has been a body?" she asked.

"No, but often no body is found. The tide."

"I see. What did he tell you of the book from New England?"

"He mentioned a garbled title and I asked him if he was referring to *Of Evill Sorceries done in New-England of Daemons in no Humane Shape*. He said yes and that he had seen the manuscript in your library."

"To whom have you communicated this information?"

A muffled explosion rent the sky. "No one. If you are in possession of the *New Dunnich Manuscript* I should very much like to see it for myself. I have a small official capacity in the Literary and Philosophical Society and I can offer *The Letters of Reverend Dyer* in exchange."

"I am not interested in the letters of a lunatic."

"But I have collected all five, as well as the letter from Reverend Conybeare."

Mrs Potter reached her left hand behind the desk panel and rang a bell. "Good day, Mr Langham, Whateley will see you out."

I stared at her without moving.

She broke the silence. "There is a storm coming. I suggest you make haste."

The female Whateley arrived. I rose from the settee and followed her out.

VII

The thunder brought a translucent white haze with it rather than snow or rain and visibility was once again reduced. There was undoubtedly a tension in the air, but my aged joints made no protest. The wagonette was waiting for me, having been turned to face the exit, and the horse was nervous and skittish. I saw the male Whateley shambling off into the mist. As I mounted, the first flash of lightning illuminated the sky, several miles to the south. I unhooked the reins, cracked the whip, and set off. I had no desire to drive all the way back to Goathland in the storm. I was not particularly concerned about the lightning, but the snow would surely resume its descent shortly and even if it didn't, the haze was damp and would leave me soaked through long before I reached the hotel. Fletcher had given me the key to the vicarage, which I had been unable to use due to the male Whateley's interruption of my investigations. I would proceed there now, find an outbuilding to shelter the horse, and take refuge from the storm. While I was there, I could also keep an eye on the church, although I had no intention of disrupting any ceremonies that unfolded.

Once I was through the trees, I felt the wind and wrapped my scarf around my face again. There was another muffled explosion behind me – followed by a moment of brightness – as if the storm was descending on Billington Manor. I arrived at the junction: right through the hamlet to civilization, straight ahead to the vicarage. I flicked my whip, but the sound was drowned by a deafening discharge of lightning. The horse took fright, reared up, and a gust of wind dispersed the mist. Fifty yards ahead, I saw a line of two dozen-odd men, women, and children. They were swaying in perfect unison and uttering a low, rhythmic chant.

The half-light of the dark day disappeared in a brilliant flash of energy as a bolt struck the earth off to my left. In the moment of illumination, I saw that every villager was holding a weapon, mostly agricultural implements or household tools. The horse lurched forward. I dropped the whip, slammed on the brake, and grabbed the reins in both hands. There was no way I'd be able to turn the wagonette around with the animal in a frenzy. It reared up again, kicking the air in a gesture both futile and frantic.

Thunder boomed directly overhead, there was another brilliant flash, and an explosion flung me from my seat.

I was knocked over the backrest into the wagonette, the smell of burned flesh and melting metal filling my nostrils. When I lifted myself up, I saw the horse had been struck by lightning. Its flesh smouldered and sizzled as the metal bit melted into its jaw. The animal had died instantly. I retrieved my stick and jumped down from the wagon as quickly as I could, which – for a man in his fifties who has not enjoyed robust health – was not very fast at all. A lightning bolt burst in the air, this one above the vicarage. Without looking back at the villagers, I staggered off into the haze.

I reached the junction, turned left, and made haste. Thunder rolled, roared, and rumbled. In the heavens, Donar – Thor to the Vikings – beat hammer against anvil. The sky bellowed, the earth shook, fiery sparks flew, and I cowered beneath the clouds as I pushed on.

After a minute, I glanced back. I couldn't see anyone behind me. Two minutes later I was through the tiny cluster of houses and approaching the first bend in the path. The slope seemed steeper than on my arrival and the snow underfoot made the going more difficult. I was breathing heavily by the time I approached the last two houses in the hamlet. The thunder was continuous, but I had left the lightning behind. One more slope to ascend, one final turn to the right, then Pike Hill Moss would be in sight. I increased my pace, pushing hard on my stick.

I rounded the bend and met the rest of the villagers.

Another two dozen men, women, and children, carrying flails, rakes, crooks, sickles, billhooks, knives, hammers, and pans. They were less than twenty yards away through the haze, swaying and chanting.

"*Eh-ya-ya-ya-yahaah, e'yayayayaaa!*"

I halted.

"*Cthuga!*"

I turned around.

"*Ngh'aaaaa, ngh'aaa, ngh'aa!*"

I could see no one behind me, but I knew the others were coming.

"*Cthuga!*"

I turned back to the line and felt nauseous as I realised that every one of them shared the Whateleys' blood. Fathers and daughters, mothers and sons, brothers and sisters... generation after generation, generation into generation... the result stretched out before me.

"*H'yuh, h'yuh, h'yuh...*"

There was a flash of light from above the line of villagers.

"*...Cthuga!*"

A ball of flame with the circumference of a wagon wheel streaked through the sky towards me. I saw two hollow eyes and a gaping mouth in the fire, but it may just have been fancy. I let go of my Penang-lawyer, the fireball struck the stick and metal and wood exploded, throwing me into the air once again. I landed in the snow at the side of the path, breathless and stunned. A second later, I realised my right glove and sleeve were on fire and rolled on top of them, rubbing them into the icy powder. I lay prone, gasping for breath, the smell of smoke thick in my nostrils.

"*Eh-ya-ya-ya-yahaah, e'yayayayaaa!*"

Slowly, the crowd of villagers shambled forward. I did not have the strength to rise.

"*Cthuga!*"

Another flash of light from above them.

I closed my eyes and awaited the impact.

"*Ngh'aaaaa, ngh'aaa –* "

I heard shouts, the neighing of a horse, a gunshot.

Definitely a gunshot, definitely not thunder or lightning.

I opened my eyes and saw that the bright light wasn't another ball of lightning, but the sun breaking through the clouds. A horseman surged through the line, scattering villagers before him. He fired in the air a second time and even the most resolute cast their weapons away and fled. It was Fletcher, mounted on a black steed, reins between his teeth, a revolver in one hand and the Elder Sign in the other.

I scrambled to my feet.

As he closed on me, the sun was eclipsed, the heavens opened, and there was an almighty crack. A flickering fork of electricity struck him. I threw up my arms for protection, but there was no explosion. The blue fire simply disappeared into Fletcher's left hand. I saw a fistful of dust spray the air as he rode past. Fletcher fired over his head once more, tucked his revolver into his belt, and turned his horse. He broke into a trot, reached down to heave me up behind him, and kicked his heels into the horse's flanks. As we approached the moss, the thunder began to fade. By the time we had rattled over the bridge, it could barely be heard in the distance. When we reached the road to Goathland, snowflakes began to fall again.

VIII

I had taken possession of Fletcher's trunk on Thursday, when it had finally arrived from the Pacific. Had I known that it contained his New Army and Navy Colt revolver, I would have demanded that he relinquish the firearm and things might not have gone so well for us in Great Billington, Elder Sign or not. Fletcher could never explain why he had stolen a horse and followed me, only that he heard the thunder and had a premonition of death, which is hardly surprising given his brother's fate. As soon as we reached Goathland, I sent a telegram to the Commissioner of the Metropolitan Police, hoping the use of my former rank would produce a rapid response. That same evening, a squad of heavily-armed policemen arrived with a troop of Yorkshire Hussars and a tall, corpulent old gentleman from London. They set off into the night and rounded up all but eight of the villagers after a brief skirmish. A battalion of Green Howards arrived at dawn on Sunday and spent the next three days hunting the fugitives down. Seven were killed while resisting arrest. The charred remains of the eighth, believed to be Mrs Potter, were found near Russell's Wood. The official verdict was self-immolation, but other rumours persisted. By Christmas, Great Billington had been razed to the ground and erased from official maps. Little Billington and Billington remain, both in the county of Bedfordshire, but there is no more Great Billington. There is only a barren lowland the locals call Devil's Hollow.

8. The Wolf Month

A Langham & Fletcher adventure

"Your average apparition can't even touch you, let alone draw blood."

Detective Fièvre, no date

I

My young friend Wilfrid Fletcher had been sharing my lodgings for less than a year when the curse that had decimated the male line of his family seemed set to turn on the female. At the end of August, The Right Honourable Mrs William Craven, née Agnes Fletcher, informed her brother of a strange and disturbing death in the village of Appletreewick. Three weeks later, a telegram arrived from Parcevall Hall with intelligence of a second attack. Neither Fletcher nor I hesitated. We made our divers preparations and left early the next morning, proceeding from the little port of Whitby to the scene of the violence as fast as our feet, a locomotive, and a horse and trap would carry us. It was these circumstances that brought us to the public bar of the Old Inn, in Appletreewick, early in the afternoon of Friday September 20th.

The room was cramped and the dark wood of the counter, floor, benches, and stools scuffed and stained with age. There were no cushions, carpets, or other comforts, but there was no dust or dirt either and for all its age and austerity, the hostelry was clearly well-managed. I could hear the sound of patrons having lunch in the adjoining dining room so I rapped on the counter with my stick. While we waited, I examined the only ornament in the room, a posed photograph of a troop of cavalrymen from the late war. I was about to make an observation to Fletcher when a tall, straight-backed man with a bushy moustache and receding hairline limped through the archway behind the bar.

"Afternoon, gentlemen, what can I get you?"

"Good afternoon. My name is Langham and this is Mr Fletcher. Did you receive our telegram?"

"I did. I have a brace of rooms ready. There wasn't any mention of lunch, but I can rustle up a ploughman's for you. My name's Wainwright, by the way, Winston Wainwright."

"Thank you, but luncheon won't be necessary. Mr Fletcher is the brother of Mrs Craven, of Parcevall Hall, and it is at her bequest that we are here. Would you mind if we asked you a few questions about the incident on Wednesday night?"

"I'm on my own today – the girl hasn't come in. If I answer your questions now, do you mind seeing yourselves up to the rooms?" When we both nodded our assent, he continued. "Would you like a drink while we talk? I won't indulge myself until the wound heals."

"Alcohol doesn't agree with me and I don't want to put you to the trouble of making coffee."

"Mr Fletcher?" he asked.

"I don't like to drink alone. I find it breeds bad habits."

"Why don't we all have a ginger beer?" asked Wainwright. He reached under the counter and brought up three bottles of Old Jamaica. "Is the bottle all right? Good."

He twisted off the caps and placed two bottles on the counter. Then he took the third for himself, lifted up the hatch, and limped into the taproom. He winced as he sat on the oak settle, shifting his weight until he was comfortable. Fletcher and I sat at the bar, on two stools. I sipped my fiery brew as Fletcher spoke.

"A few weeks ago, Mrs Craven notified me that a man had been savaged to death in the village. Yesterday, she telegrammed to say that you'd been attacked the night before. I am well aware of the local lore, that Troller's Gill is home to the barghest; I am also aware that despite this lore, the black dog has not bitten anyone for hundreds of years. May I ask what befell you the night before last?"

Wainwright waved his empty hand. "You need not be concerned about my state of mind, Mr Fletcher. I am a Dalesman, it's true, and like every other Dalesman I know that the barghest lives in Hell Hole in the gill and roams abroad on a night. I know that to see it is bad luck and that to be followed by it means you'd better put your affairs in order, but I spent two years in the Imperial Yeomanry and the only creature I fear at night is man; a man with a rifle who knows how to use it. I wasn't attacked by a ghost dog." He placed his beer bottle on the seat next to him, reached down to his right boot, and raised the trouser leg to his knee. Most of his shin was covered with a bandage, which was stained red, orange, and yellow, particularly towards the back, at the calf. "I'm not to take the dressing off until this evening, but it's a bite, a dirty great big bite."

Wainwright replaced his trouser leg, took a draft from his drink, and continued. "When I need rabbits for the pot, I hunt them after dark. I don't have time during the day and it keeps my night vision sharp. I was on Ap'trick pasture by about half-nine – I don't like to leave it too late so as not to disturb folks' sleep –

when I saw something big moving in the moonlight. It came out of Tarn Ghyll Wood and headed straight for me. I dropped to one knee and gave it three shots. When the third made no impact, I turned and ran. I was two hundred yards from the parsonage and I thought it was my best chance."

"You thought you'd outrun an animal?" asked Fletcher.

"No, but it was still over four hundred yards away and there wasn't any point in pouring more lead into it."

"Good Lord," I cut in, "do you mean to tell us you hunt rabbits with a .303!"

"I do. I have to chop them up anyway and the round saves me from having to search for shotgun pellets and saves my customers from breaking their teeth when I miss one."

"You must be a very accurate shot," I replied.

"I am. Are you a military man, Mr Langham?"

"Many years ago. You knew that you'd hit the beast at least once and that it had made no difference?"

"I knew I'd hit it three times – it was as big as a cow and running straight towards me – downhill too. If my aim was that bad, I'd never have made it back to the Dales from the *veldt*."

"Pray continue," I replied.

"I was about twenty yards away from the parsonage wall when I heard a growl close by. I kept going, but it hit me from behind, teeth sinking into my leg. I fell a few feet from the wall, turned, and saw the beast rearing to strike again. I fired into its jaws, dropped the rifle, and dragged myself into the parsonage. And that was all. It didn't follow me and when Mr Haig and me returned it was gone."

"You said it was the size of a cow. Can you provide any more detail?" asked Fletcher.

"I think it was a wolf, but it was a much bigger wolf

than any I've heard of. Other than the size, the only unusual thing was its eyes. They seemed too big for its face and they were red. There was one more thing too."

"What was that?"

"There was no blood, not a drop. Not next to my rifle and not on the path it took when it charged."

II

Less than two hours after hearing Wainwright's remarkable tale, Fletcher and I were seated in the parsonage with pots of tea and coffee provided by the curate, Reverend Haig. He was a small man in his forties, with grey hair and a deep scar across his chin. The parsonage was rather luxurious when compared with the plain, functional church whose roof was adorned with a cross that looked like it had been plucked from a graveyard. Haig had received us in his parlour, which showed signs of a woman's touch, and left us to prepare our own drinks. He returned a few minutes later, sat in the armchair closest to the fireplace, and poured himself a cup of tea.

"I do apologise, gentlemen, I thought we had digestive biscuits, but the larder is rather bare at the moment. We've not quite recovered from the shock yet. I understand you are Mrs Craven's brother, Mr Fletcher?"

"I have that honour."

"Indeed, a most exemplary young lady, already one of those pillars of the community one hears so much about yet meets so rarely in the flesh. Mr Craven spends a great deal of his time on government duties, but Mrs Craven's energy and enthusiasm is such that his absence is barely noticed."

"Agnes wrote to me about the death of your man last month and when Wainwright was attacked, I came as quickly as I could. We have just been to the inn, where we heard his tale. He strikes me as a very reliable witness."

"Oh, more than that, he has nerves of steel. And once he's recovered, he's the man we need to hunt this monster."

"You refer to his war service in the Imperial Yeomanry?" I asked.

"Yes, he's an expert horseman and a crack shot. He was highly decorated, you know, and would have been commissioned had he not opted to return here. The inn is the family business."

Fletcher said, "Does that mean we can take his word as... oh, I was going to say *gospel*, I'm so sorry."

"Never mind, no offence taken and yes, I would trust him with my life and I was witness to at least some of his story. My wife and I heard the shots clearly and a minute later Wainwright was hammering on our door. His right calf had been badly bitten. I administered what medical attention I could. Then I gave him poor Postlewhite's shotgun, armed myself with a spade, and ventured out into the night. There was a blood trail from my front door to the east wall. His rifle was lying on the other side of the wall, where there was more blood."

Fletcher frowned. "Wainwright said there was no blood on that side of the wall."

"I assume he meant the monster's. The blood I saw was his – the trail from my door went over the wall and stopped a few yards on the other side."

"Were there any tracks?"

"Not that I could see."

"Could you tell us about Postlewhite's death?"

"Certainly. It was on Friday 23rd August, exactly four weeks ago. He was returning from the Old Inn after closing time – a little the worse for wear, I expect, though I said nothing to his wife – and took the shortcut from Main Street to the servants' quarters at the back. The route passes through a small grove, which is where the thing was waiting for him. He screamed and tried to run, but it caught him and... well, tore his throat out, ripped an ear and part of his face off, and broke both of his arms in several places." Haig shook his head slowly. "The only consolation is that his death was quick, albeit horrible."

"Who found the body?" asked Fletcher.

"I did. I heard the screams, realised he was dead, and ran back to prevent Mrs Postlewhite from seeing him in that state."

"You didn't see the beast?"

"Thankfully not."

"Was anything done about it?"

"Not really. A police inspector arrived from Skipton, decided a wolf had killed him, and sent some constables to the local farms and manors to alert them."

"Wolves have been extinct in England for nearly five hundred years," I said.

"I know," Haig replied, "and they hunt in packs, but I couldn't convince the police otherwise."

"What do you think it was?" asked Fletcher.

"I think it is some sort of prehistoric wolf – like *Canis dirus* in the Americas – that's survived beyond the extinction of its species. This sort of thing happens all the time with marine species so there's no reason it shouldn't occur on land. The limestone in the Dales is famous for its underground caverns, pots, and gills, which may explain why the continued existence of this particular species has remained a secret. Or at least an open secret because this is of course the home of Yorkshire's own black dog, the barghest. But it was no ghost dog that tore Postlewhite to pieces or savaged Wainwright. No, the real question is why it's started attacking now."

"Do you have the answer?"

"Only a theory. Two months ago a cave-hunter named Cording disappeared. His last known whereabouts were Kettlewell, but Wainwright had seen a man of his description here a few weeks before the police began making enquiries. I think he blundered into the wrong cave, was killed by the wolf, and gave it a taste for human flesh. We are, after all, much easier to catch than sheep, even if we do put up more of a fight once caught."

Fletcher nodded. "That sounds plausible. If you're right, then the beast will have to be killed. I'm sure Agnes will assist in recruiting a band to hunt it down once Wainwright has returned to full health."

"I think that would be the best course of action."

III

We declined Haig's kindly offer to escort us to the scene of both attacks. There was no urgency to inspect the first, which was already four weeks old, and Fletcher and I were due at Parcevall Hall. With respect to the second, I have always found it better to approach the scene of a violent event with a fresh pair of eyes – even in cases such as this, where the Reverend had washed the blood away, being unaware of Mrs Craven's summons. Fletcher and I retraced Wainwright's flight from the drystone wall to the parsonage. There was a large oak tree in the corner of the property, with a gate in the wall to the north that gave access onto the slopes of Whithill, rising to the north-east and known locally as Ap'trick pasture. The Hall was at the top of hill, about a mile and a half away, sheltered behind Tarn Ghyll Wood. While I examined the stone on this side of the eastern wall, Fletcher used the gate to walk around to the other.

Despite the absence of mortar, drystone walls in the Dales were notoriously robust and there was no evidence of Wainwright's passage. I knelt and took a closer look at the stones whereupon I was able to discern a few stains that had resisted Haig's cleansing.

I joined Fletcher on the far side, where the ground was at a lower level than the churchyard. He was squatting down, examining the wall. "Have you found anything?"

"Some stains between the stones that Haig missed. That's all – wait, what's this!"

"What is it?" I asked as I knelt next to him. He removed a tiny pair of pincers from one pocket and a handkerchief from another. Reaching the tip of the pincers into a gap in the stones, he extracted a clump of black hair. He placed it on his handkerchief and handed it to me. I poked it with my finger and raised it to my nose before handing it back. "It has the texture of fur and smells of wet dog."

Fletcher stood and sniffed the evidence. "Is it from a wolf?"

"I have no idea. It might well be from a sheepdog, although the fibres do seem coarser and thicker than I'd expect." I inspected the ground immediately in front of the wall. There were no signs of the struggle that had taken place two days before. There were two small stands of trees obscuring our view to the north, but by following the line of those trees we could walk up the slope towards the wood.

"Shall we continue retracing Wainwright's steps?" I suggested. "We can walk up to the Hall that way." Fletcher nodded and we set off. "Are you sure you wouldn't rather remain there after dinner?"

"No, both attacks have been closer to the village and Agnes has a sizeable staff to hand. She also has an elephant gun from her father-in-law's collection, a great old Holland & Holland double four-bore, which should keep us safe on the return journey."

"The crucial question is whether the four-bore *will* provide us with protection."

"Surely you don't believe in the barghest?"

"You and I have both been witness to terrible things," I said softly.

Fletcher turned pale and he swallowed before answering. "Ghost dogs don't leave tufts of hair as evidence of their passing nor do they savage their prey with such visceral ferocity."

"I grant you the former, but I am not so sure of the latter. I have heard it said that the ability of an apparition, phantom, or spectre to contact the living is dependent upon the strength of belief in its existence – a similar idea to the old myth that faith lends substance."

"So the more people who believe in a ghost the more damage the ghost can do?"

"The more people who believe in a ghost the more corporeality it assumes, from sight to sound, smell, touch, and taste."

"And when its touch can be felt, it can cause harm?"

I shrugged. "I think that's the general conception, yes. Granted, a ghost dog seems highly improbable, but why didn't Wainwright's fourth shot kill it and why didn't it follow him into the churchyard?"

"He may have missed – or just winged – it. If it is a prehistoric wolf, it would probably have been frightened by the close proximity of the explosion, which would explain its subsequent disappearance."

"Perhaps, but I am keeping an open mind because an alternative explanation of the same facts is that the ghost dog would not follow him onto holy ground."

Fletcher did not respond and we continued the next two hundred yards in silence. The scenery was typical of the Dales, with low rolling hills of different shades

of green surrounding us. The village was now behind
and below. To our left, the land was level for a few
hundred yards before sloping gently down to Barben
Beck; to our right, it rose steeply to the vantage point
known as Simon's Seat, on a rocky crag far to the
south-east. Parcevall Hall lay directly ahead, at about
half a mile distance and a dozen or so yards of
elevation, out of sight beyond Tarn Ghyll Wood.
Troller's Gill, a dry limestone valley, lay to the north of
the Hall, running along the top of Whithill, and Hell
Hole was a cave at the very end of the gill. When we
approached the point of which Wainwright had
spoken, we put some space between us and advanced
more slowly, scouring the ground in an effort to find
the cartridges from his rifle.

Although Fletcher had the better chance with his
younger eyes, I soon felt something press into the
earth under my right shoe. I halted, knelt to prise the
grass apart, and discovered a .303 shell case. "This is
one of them." I held it up to Fletcher, who glanced at it
before placing it in his waistcoat pocket.

"There's the second," he said, "and the third."

I retrieved both, passed them to him, and stood. I
looked up at the wood and imagined a large, dark form
racing towards us. It would have been unnerving
enough in the daylight and Wainwright had exhibited
exceptional composure in his decision to run when his
shots had no effect. Had he stood his ground, he may
well have met the same fate as Postlewhite.

"Shall we split up again and look for traces of
blood?" Fletcher asked.

"I don't think there's much point. Wainwright is
convinced he hit the beast four times and if there was
no blood at point blank range, we are unlikely to find
any between here and the wood."

"You are setting an unusual amount of store by
Wainwright's word."

"He strikes me as a stout fellow, physically and mentally, but perhaps my liking has clouded my judgement."

Fletcher shook his head. "No, you are probably right – there is little to be gained and I am anxious to see Agnes."

We resumed our earlier pace, walking side by side, and continued up the slope. The wood was composed of pines for the most part, with firs scattered here and there. No sooner had we set foot in the sylvan sanctuary than the quiet was rent by a roar, thundering through the trees from somewhere to our left.

Fletcher drew his New Army and Navy Colt revolver. "Do ghost dogs venture out in broad daylight?"

"Let's not wait to find out," I replied, pointing north with my stick. "The Hall – quick!"

IV

Despite our undignified and dishevelled arrival, neither the journey to nor from Parcevall Hall was eventful. We did not hear the beast again and there were no sightings at either the Hall or the village overnight. Twenty-eight hours after and one hundred yards east of where we had begun our ignominious flight, Fletcher and I found ourselves in the company of Wainwright and Haig, our foursome fully-equipped to hunt both prehistoric wolves and ghost dogs. The sky was cloudless and the moon full, but as we intended to roust the beast from its lair I carried a bullseye lantern and Haig a flaming torch. I also wielded the sword-stick that had recently been a gift from Fletcher and upon whose head I had more recently commissioned the embossing of a *tiwaz* rune. *Tiwaz* was the symbol of Týr, the Viking deity who bound Fenrir, the monstrous wolf that threatened the gods. Haig had a crucifix around his neck, three vials of holy water in his pockets, and a hunting horn slung over his shoulder. Fletcher was carrying the huge four-bore, which weighed over twenty pounds when loaded, his revolver, and a boatswain's call. Wainwright carried his .303, with a double-barrelled shotgun slung across his back, and the bayonet for the rifle in the boot of his unwounded leg.

"Are you sure you are sufficiently recovered?" I asked him.

"I took the dressing off this morning – it's nearly healed."

I wondered if he had exaggerated the extent of the wound. "Good. We have over eight hours of darkness left so there is no need to rush. The Reverend and I will lead with our lights. If our luck holds, the beast will find us. If not, Fletcher will make the descent into Hell Hole. As a last resort, we shall use the horn and the whistle to attract its attention. Are there any questions?"

There were none and I set off northward, with Haig at my side and Wainwright and Fletcher behind us. We were traversing rather than climbing Whithill and made quick progress, reaching the western edge of the Hall in a matter of minutes. The moonlight was obscured by the trees in the Hall gardens, but our lights kept the shadows at bay. Shortly, we picked up a footpath, nothing more than a track of trampled grass that had been flattened by sheep and the occasional pair of human feet. We passed a small stand of trees on the left before arriving at the entrance to the gill. Two low, scree-strewn slopes rose above four twisted trees as the path descended and turned out of sight to the right. Our visibility would be much reduced, but the loose limestone would alert us to a flank attack by a prehistoric wolf. Our lights would continue to illuminate the front when we entered the gill, leaving the rear vulnerable to attack.

"Let us switch to single-file," I suggested. "I'll lead with the lantern and the Reverend can bring up the rear with the torch."

They all nodded and Fletcher fell in behind me as I made for the gap in the hawthorns. The trees appeared to have been warped by the wind, though the night was completely calm, and the branches and leaves formed an arch that temporarily hid the moon's radiance. I had just crossed the threshold of the gill, re-emerging into the light, when I heard the same booming roar I had heard previously, echoing off the sides of the outcrops ahead. I stopped and glanced over my shoulder. Fletcher was behind me, Haig behind him, and Wainwright under the trees. The roar came again and I took another step forward – we had, after all, come to find the thing, whatever it was. The second roar was still echoing from the gill when the third began. I raised the lantern and was about to step up my pace when I heard Haig call out from behind. Fletcher and I turned at the same time.

Haig and Wainwright were both under the hawthorn arch, but the former had thrown his torch on the ground and was hovering about the latter, who was on his knees, bent double. As I handed Fletcher my lantern, Wainwright howled in agony, hunching over so that he was on all fours.

Haig grabbed him by the shoulders. "What is it, man, what is it!"

Wainwright's back burst through his coat. Haig screamed and Wainwright raised a head that was half-human, half-animal: covered in black hair, unnaturally elongated, teeth too big for the mouth. With lightning speed and supernatural strength, he leaped up, grabbed Haig with what were now claws, and buried his jaws in his neck. I knew Fletcher couldn't fire the elephant gun without cutting Haig in half so I swivelled the handle of my stick, cast the scabbard aside, and lunged for Wainwright's kidneys. The sword glanced off to the right, causing me to lose my balance. It was if I'd tried to drive it into a brick wall. Wainwright threw Haig's body to the ground and turned to me, his limbs hideously lengthened and hairy, his eyes shining red.

I heard Fletcher from behind: "Langham, move!"

I jumped away, narrowly avoiding a bolt of flame as an explosion deafened me. Fletcher fired the first barrel of the four-bore and then the second, but the big bullets did no damage to Wainwright. Fletcher cursed. Wainwright sprang at me, his bloody maw open. I offered him my left hand and drew back the sword for another strike, in a desperate bid to replicate the binding of Fenrir. Fangs sliced through the flesh and bone of my forearm. I screamed, dropped my sword, and fell. My clumsiness saved me as Wainwright's jaws snapped at the empty space where my head had been. I landed on my back, felt his fangs tear through my left shoulder, and saw him draw back for the *coup de grâce*.

I heard a shot, looked at Fletcher, and saw him fire two more above his head. Wainwright turned and crouched for a giant leap.

Fletcher pointed the revolver at him and fired once. The bullet thumped into his chest and he convulsed. Fletcher fired again. The shot caught Wainwright between his red eyes, his head snapped back, and he toppled over, limp and lifeless. Fletcher advanced, revolver pointed at the monstrous hybrid.

I clutched my bleeding arm to my stomach and tried to roll onto my torn shoulder to staunch the flow of blood.

Fletcher fired his last shot into Wainwright's head,

which was resuming its former shape, then dashed over to Haig.

In a few seconds he was at my side, the revolver set down as he made a tourniquet with his belt. "Haig's dead."

"What did you do?" I asked through clenched teeth.

"I considered a third possibility: ghost dog, prehistoric wolf, or werewolf. I had six silver bullets made while you were having your stick embossed."

He tightened the belt on my elbow, told me to hold the end, and left. He returned with a piece of Wainwright's shirt, which he used as a bandage for my shoulder.

"I hope you have a silver bullet left," I said.

"Three, why?"

"For me. Do it now."

V

Fletcher did not kill me then and had no need to later. His immediate aid prevented me from losing too much blood until I could be treated by a doctor, who set my broken wrist and stitched my wounded forearm and shoulder. Fletcher and I left the Dales for a sanatorium in York, where he sat with me through the next full moon and the one after. Neither of us is sure why the disease that was transmitted to Wainwright was not transmitted to me. My best guess is that the homicidal somnambulism from which I had suffered two decades before was a form of lycanthropy and that having survived it I had acquired a certain immunity. Alternatively, the rune may have had some power. While Fletcher sat at my bedside with a vial of carbolic acid in one pocket and his revolver with the silver bullets in the other, the Craven district was patrolled by the officers and men of the 9th Yorkshire (West

Riding) Rifle Volunteer Corps from Skipton. The Right Honourable William Craven paid for a company of hunters, cavers, and half-pay officers to scour Troller's Gill, Hell Hole, Grimwith Fell, and The Devil's Apronful. They found no evidence of a large predator. The barghest has been seen abroad since, but has taken no more victims, and Fletcher and I decided that the truth was best kept from the public at large. Notwithstanding, the blacksmith at Appletreewick has become well-known as both an ironmonger and a silversmith.

9. The Christmas Cracker

A Ghost Story

"There may be possibilities, too, in the Christmas cracker, if the right people pull it, and if the motto which they find inside has the right message on it."

M.R. James, 1929

I

The internal architecture of No. 10 Flowergate is rather unusual. For one, the ground floor consists of a single large room, apportioned to a reception area, dining-room, and sitting-room-cum-library with the strategic deployment of furniture. For another, the kitchen is on the first floor, although the inconvenience is compensated for by the presence of a water-closet. Both are the result of the idiosyncrasy of a former owner; the conversion of the small drawing-room into a study that of the current owner. The second floor is also out of the ordinary, comprising two bedrooms of ample and equal size, one which overlooks the front of the premises and the other the rear. The domicile is thus perfectly suited to the pleasant cohabitation of two independent gentlemen and it was this consideration amongst others that had prompted me to invite Mr Wilfrid Fletcher to take up residence there. I have recounted the curious circumstances of our meeting elsewhere and I shall only say, by way of introduction, that his health had recovered fully and that he was gainfully employed as the Under-Sheriff of Whitby by the time of our second Christmas together in 1908. Fletcher had suggested that I invite Largo Delapena, the flamboyant American editor of the *Dailygraph*, to join us for Christmas dinner – which was how I came to be opening the door to that very gentleman at eight o'clock *post meridiem*.

"Mr Delapena, do come in out of the snow."

He was a slim man of medium height, with a somewhat ghastly pallor to his flesh that was accentuated by the fact that he was always clad in black from head to foot. His hair was worn rather longer than fashionable, his moustache rather smaller than fashionable, and his clothes harked back to an earlier era, including a top hat, Ascot Tie in the Regency style, and a cape to keep off the snow. Although we had never met, I had seen Delapena many times, usually carousing in the public bar of the Royal Hotel, and I wasn't sure if he was my own age, mid-fifties, or younger but looking older. Both the darkness and abundance of his brown hair also muddied the waters in this regard. The bags under his eyes spoke of lack of sleep, profusion of alcohol, or a combination of the two, and I had indeed never seen him without a drink in his hand.

"Good evening, sir!"

I took his hat, stick, cape, and gloves and then offered my hand. "I cannot recall that we have ever been introduced. My name is Roderick Langham and this is my particular friend, Mr Wilfrid Fletcher."

He shook hands with both of us. "Delighted, delighted. I know Mr Fletcher better as the Under-Sheriff, but I confess I know very little about you, sir, except that you frequent the Royal Hotel every

Wednesday night and are associated with the Literary and Philosophical Society."

"I imagine nothing gets past you in your capacity as editor of the *Dailygraph*, Mr Delapena, but I see that you are also a keen observer of your fellow man."

He waved graciously. "There's no need for formalities, Mr Langham, no need."

"In that case, may I ask your indulgence in sitting down to the dinner table at once. My housekeeper insisted on serving us and I do not want to keep her away from her kith and kin."

"What would you like to drink?" asked Fletcher.

"A glass of gin, with a little sugar and water, if I may."

"May I suggest a sloe gin, in keeping with the season?"

"Very good!"

Fletcher poured the gin for Delapena, a glass of red wine for himself, and a glass of water for me.

I raised my glass to Delapena. "To your very good health."

"My health is always excellent, sir, so allow me to drink to the health of my hosts instead."

We saluted each other and imbibed our beverages. I invited Delapena to sit at the table, took my place next to Fletcher, and rang the bell to let Mrs Knaggs know we were ready.

Delapena glanced quickly about him as he sat. "Three chairs of course, but I wonder where you have stowed the fourth?"

Our small dining table was made for four, but there were only three places set. "You really are a keen observer, aren't you?" I chuckled. "The fourth has been permanently relocated to my study. I find the hard chair assists with my back pain."

"You are a writer, sir, confess it!"

I raised my glass to him. "You have found me out."

"May I ask what you write?" Fletcher began to say something and Delapena caught his gist immediately. "I have no wish to intrude, sir; it is just that as the editor of the only daily paper hereabouts, you have made me feel something of a fool for failing to recognise your name."

I nodded my thanks to Fletcher. "Can you keep a confidence, Delapena?"

"Of course."

"I write the lurid and improbable tales of Sexton Blake."

"Ah, the *other* Baker Street detective. But I *love* a good mystery, how is it that I've not read any of your work?"

"All my writing is anonymous. I find the payment indirectly proportional to the literary merit and I confess I am somewhat ashamed of the money I have made."

"Not at all, not at all! There's nothing like a good mystery to pass the time of day. You must write something for the *Dailygraph*, Langham, you *must*. Name your price, whatever you wish – just don't let any of my staff know it!" I smiled, but did not answer and was relieved when Delapena turned his attention to the laying of the table. "A bon-bon for each of us – delightful! I do love a bon-bon at Christmas, a British tradition of which I wholeheartedly approve."

Fletcher frowned. "Excuse me, Delapena, don't you mean a cracker? I thought a bon-bon was a French cake or confection."

"Of course, of course. I have an antiquarian turn of phrase at times. They used to be called bon-bons."

"And more recently *cosaques*," I added, "Fletcher is too young to remember." Fletcher was sitting to my right so I reached across my torso with my left hand and offered my cracker to Delapena with my right. When the chain was complete, Fletcher counted down from three and our combined efforts produced three loud *pops* in very quick succession. Each tube contained a sugared almond, a motto, and a paper crown. "I don't wish to be a killjoy," I said, "but perhaps we can forego donning the crowns since there are no children present."

"Seconded, seconded. This almond is delicious! Where did you get these crackers?"

Fletcher had been responsible for the Christmas arrangements. "I had them sent up from Fortnum and Masons."

"Very good! I shall order some myself next year. Will you read your motto first?"

Fletcher unwrapped the piece of paper and read: "*Some say that ever 'gainst that season comes Wherein our Saviour's birth is celebrated, The bird of dawning singeth all night long: And then, they say, no spirit dare stir abroad; The nights are wholesome; then no planets strike, No fairy takes, nor witch hath power to charm, So hallowed and so gracious is the time.* Shakespeare. From *Hamlet*, I think."

"Yes, he describes a holy time when evil is kept without. Shall I be next?" I opened mine. "*By the pricking of my thumbs, Something wicked this way comes. Open, locks, Whoever knocks.* Still Shakespeare, but not quite in the Christmas spirit, I'm afraid. What a strange choice. It is your turn."

Delapena opened his motto and gasped. He recovered quickly, but what little colour he possessed had drained from his face, leaving the flesh a deathly grey. "Mine's very short. "*Now hast thou but one bare hour to live, And then thou must be damn'd perpetually!*"

"Well, that's in very poor taste!" cried Fletcher. "Please accept my apologies. I shall write to Fortnum and Masons and complain. Not just inappropriate, but lazy too. Three quotes from Shakespeare in a single batch."

"I agree," I said, "but that wasn't Shakespeare. It was Marlowe."

Delapena nodded slowly, still shaken. "From *Doctor Faustus*."

II

It was close to ten o'clock when I assisted Mrs Knaggs in removing the remnants of her magnificent pudding and custard along with the crockery and cutlery. I left Fletcher settling Delapena down in front of the fire with a glass of port and a cigar. He had already finished the sloe gin on his own, though he seemed none the worse for it. I had just persuaded Mrs Knaggs that it would quite all right to delay the washing up until the morning or even, heaven forbid, much later, when Fletcher appeared with a couple of empty glasses. Mrs Knaggs wished us both a good night and a merry Christmas and left the kitchen.

As soon as she began her descent, Fletcher leaned forward and whispered to me. It was quite unnecessary, but he was obviously anxious not to offend our guest. "Do you notice the resemblance!"

"To whom?"

"To Edgar Allan Poe, obviously. My God, old chap, it's not just unmistakable, it's uncanny!"

"Perhaps. I believe that Poe has inspired a number of imitators of not only his works, but his appearance and habits. Delapena may be one of them."

"If so, he's done a damned good job of it."

"Don't keep him waiting. I'm going to brew coffee. I assume you don't want any tea just yet?"

Fletcher shook his head and departed.

When I joined them shortly after, they were deep in

discussion about the scandal in the Belgian Congo. They were both drinking port and Fletcher was smoking one of his Black Russian cigarettes. I had just sat the coffee tray down on the side table when there was a knock at the door. Delapena started visibly – knocking back his port in an effort to conceal his sudden consternation. "I'll get it," I said, since I was still standing. I had no friends other than Fletcher and his social circle was almost as small so I was curious as to the identity of our interloper.

When I opened the door, no one was there. It was still snowing, although more lightly than before, and Flowergate was covered in a thick, white blanket. A couple was walking down the street, so far away that they were almost out of sight. Perhaps it was someone making mischief, someone who had knocked on the door and then bolted up Cliff Street, but when I looked at the pavement outside the door there were no footprints. I returned to the fire.

"Who was it?" asked Delapena, his visage grim, grey, and lined.

"No one. Well, someone must have knocked, but there was no one there when I answered. You aren't expecting anyone, are you, Delapena?"

"Of course not, what do you take me for!"

"Do excuse me," I replied, "I meant no offence."

"Nevermind, nevermind. My fault entirely. I was just a little startled."

I sat down in my chair, poured myself a cup of coffee, and began packing my pipe.

There were a few seconds of uncomfortable silence, which Fletcher broke. "I say, Delapena, would you mind if I asked you a personal question?"

"Not at all, not at all; help yourself, young sir."

Fletched cleared his throat. "I was wondering if you were by any chance related to Edgar Allan Poe?"

Delapena nearly choked on his port and I had to

rescue it while he coughed and spluttered. Fletcher rose to his assistance and offered a handkerchief.

"I am sorry, Delapena, I had no wish to alarm you!"

Delapena coughed again, tears running from the corner of his eyes, and laughed, the sound high in pitch and unsteady in tone. "No, no, you just made me laugh so much I could not control myself. Poe, the poet! Really, Fletcher, what do you take me for – his son?"

Fletcher frowned. "No, you'd have to be his grandson. He died fifty years ago, I think, or perhaps sixty."

Delapena chuckled, more evenly this time, and took charge of his port again. Fletcher refilled his glass and I noticed the bottle was nearly empty. He still showed no signs of intoxication.

"Poe died without any offspring," I said. "I believe he never recovered from the death of his wife and his commercial publishing ventures were entirely unsuccessful. His end was rather tragic, I'm afraid."

Delapena picked up on my point about publishing and commerce and we soon left the topic of Poe behind.

III

The clock struck eleven and Delapena excused himself to perform his ablutions upstairs. As soon as he was gone, Fletcher leaned forward. "I didn't mean to upset him, but I'm sure about the resemblance." He leaped to his feet. "Tell me if you hear him coming back. Where is your Poe?" I had acquired all four volumes of the Ingram edition of *The Works of Edgar Allan Poe* for my modest library. "Here we are, *Volume I – Tales* will suffice. Aha, just as I thought. Look at the frontispiece, the photograph!"

Fletcher was right. The likeness was indeed remarkable and except for the white shirt and light coloured overcoat Poe wore for his sitting, the man represented in the photograph looked very much like our guest. "Do you not think Poe slightly fuller in the face than Delapena?" I asked.

"I do not! Even if he is, the hair, the eyes, the moustache – it's his twin!"

"Or his doppelganger if you have read Poe's 'William Wilson'."

"Should I show him the photograph?" asked Fletcher.

"No, not after his reaction when you suggested a familial relationship. Also, if I remember correctly, 'William Wilson' does not end well for the protagonist. Poe's stories seldom do." I heard the creak of floorboards above. "Quick, put the book back!"

Fletcher did so, but Delapena returned to silence.

"Don't allow me to interrupt, gentlemen, pray continue with your conversation."

Fletcher gaped for a moment, saw *The Journal of Philosophy, Psychology and Scientific Methods* I had placed in the bookrack, and said: "Darwin. Evolution and all that."

I had to prevent myself from smiling because Fletcher's chain of thought was so transparent. Our clandestine conversation was about Poe. Fletcher's favourite of Poe's tales was "The Murders in the Rue Morgue". The antagonist in that particular story is an Ourang-Outang, which according to Mr Darwin was one of the apes from which human beings have evolved. In his panic to find a topic of conversation, Fletcher's gaze had alighted on my *Journal*. We had recently had a discussion about an article called "The Evolution of Pragmatism" which, as its title suggests, is about pragmatism rather than evolution. With Poe and his ape in mind, however, Fletcher had recalled the title and proceeded directly to Darwin.

The ruse seemed to work and any awkwardness was avoided. Fletcher had just lit Delapena's second cigar with a lucifer when there was another knock at the door.

Delapena's head swivelled so quickly I thought he must do himself an injury.

"My turn," said Fletcher, who was still on his feet. He extinguished the lucifer, dropped it in the ash-receiver, and proceeded to the door.

In order to prevent the escape of all the warm air, I had positioned a Welsh dresser and a pair of bookcases between the dining table and reception area, a strategy that had the added advantage of maintaining the privacy of the library. As soon as he realised this, Delapena ceased craning his neck and turned back to me. "Evolution, huh. That reminds me of your young friend's mention of Poe. What do you make of him – as a writer, that is – from one author to another?"

I could not help but smile this time, the chain of thought coming full circle. "I make no pretensions as an author, Delapena, but I am, I hope, a careful and considerate reader. Mr James Russell Lowell provided an excellent thumb-nail sketch when he..." The door shut and Fletcher joined us. "...Who was it?" I asked.

"I don't know. There was no one there." He seemed rather more disturbed than one would expect.

"You seem to be prone to pranksters, gentlemen, that must be it." Delapena puffed on his cigar, his equanimity apparently restored.

I thought the notion unlikely myself, but did not want to upset him. "Yes, you must be right. Perhaps someone of whom Fletcher has made an enemy in his official capacity." Fletcher raised his eyebrows as he sat down and reached for his drink. I continued before he could contradict me. "Delapena was just asking me my opinion of Poe and I was about to quote Lowell. Do you know that Lowell was a regular visitor here?" I asked Delapena.

"I do, in fact. Only because I took an interest in his poetry, of course," he added hastily. "Did you ever meet him?"

"No, he had been dead several years before I moved here. Are you familiar with any of Lowell's work?" I asked Fletcher.

"I had no idea he was a poet, but I knew of him as the American ambassador, from 1880 or so onwards, I think."

"One of the Fireside Poets of the last century, with Longfellow and a few others. I have several of his volumes. To return to your original question, Delapena, I think it's in *A Fable for Critics* that he writes: *Here comes Poe with his raven, like Barnaby Rudge Three fifths of him genius and two fifths sheer fudge*. I have not read all of Poe's *oeuvre*, but Lowell's rhyme certainly captures my opinion of what I have read."

Delapena smiled and nodded. "Very good, Langham, very good! Three fifths genius and two fifths fudge. Any man should be pleased with such an epitaph."

"And what about you" asked Fletcher, "what do you make of Poe as an author?"

"I think he was lacking in foresight."

"Foresight? How so?"

"He did not, for example, think that his *tales of ratiocination* as he called them would prove more than a passing fad. If they are indeed a fad, they are a fad that has lasted more than six decades and shows no signs of abating. Am I not right, Langham?"

I laughed. "Quite so, but please don't put my potboilers in the same category as Poe's detective stories. I assure you, they are entirely lacking in merit, literary or otherwise."

"I am sure you are too modest and poor old Poe could have escaped the poverty of his last days had he made more accurate an estimate of the demand for the tale of detection. As it was...hard times, hard times indeed. Yes, *he* fell into despair, but I think he would have been content had he known his legacy would be three fifths genius – *I* would have been."

For the next three quarters of an hour we dissertated on the merits of the various writers of detective stories since Poe.

IV

The clock began striking midnight.

"Is that the time already? I fear I am abusing your hospitality, gentlemen."

"Certainly not, Delapena. Fletcher and I are solitary and serious-minded individuals and it is a rare treat for us to entertain so stimulating a guest. We have no need to rise early, so why not stay a while? I shall attend to the fire, Fletcher will pour you another drink, and you can light another cigar while we are so engaged."

As Fletcher and I rose, he said, "Remind me to attend to the clock, tomorrow."

I opened my watch. "It is keeping good time."

"Yes, but it just struck thirteen."

When we had resumed our places with cigar, cigarette, and pipe alight and port poured for Delapena and Fletcher, the former resumed. "My favourite Poe tale is not in fact one of his tales of ratiocination, but a comedy, a farce even. Have either of you read "Bon-Bon"? I thought not. It is a rewrite of one of his earliest efforts, "The Bargain Lost", and was first published in the *Southern Literary Messenger*. It concerns a pompous French chef and self-proclaimed philosopher by the name of Pierre Bon-Bon. One night while working on one of his expositions, the philosopher is visited by the devil in the form of a tall, lean man wearing green spectacles. He and Bon-Bon begin drinking, with the chef becoming very drunk as the devil regales him with stories of all the different souls he has eaten. The devil then pulls out a signed agreement where, for great mental endowments and a great sum of money, a celebrated luminary has signed his soul over. Bon-Bon is instantly attracted by this bargain and offers his own soul. Luckily for him, the devil is a gentleman and refuses to take advantage of a drunkard. The tale ends with the drunken philosopher-chef collapsing on his floor, his soul safe."

"Forgive me," said Fletcher, "but that does not sound like a very substantial story. With so much to choose from in Poe, I am surprised you value it so. What, may I ask, is the appeal?"

"Oh, it is purely personal. The optimism of the man to think that the devil would not do a deal with a drunkard. As I said, Poe was lacking in foresight. Would you excuse me a moment?"

Delapena rested his cigar on the edge of the ash-receiver and ascended the stairs. His need of the water-closet was not unexpected; he had consumed the better part of the two bottles of port he and Fletcher had shared, in addition to the bottle of sloe gin. As soon as we heard his footsteps overhead, Fletcher leaned forward again.

"What happened when you answered the door?"

"There was no one there. The street was empty."

"Were there any footprints near the door?" I shook my head. "This is all very strange, Langham."

"Fetch that Poe, again, will you. Does it say when he was born?"

Fletcher had the volume open in a trice. "January the nineteenth, 1809."

"I thought so. His centenary is less than four weeks away."

Fletcher returned the volume to its place and resumed his seat. "Why do you ask?"

"I cannot quite say."

We heard Delapena's tread again and when he reappeared, we were discussing the merits of Shakespeare's comedies over his tragedies.

Delapena sat down, drew on his cigar, and had a long draught from the port glass Fletcher had refilled from a new bottle.

There was a hammering at the door – three hard knocks, much louder than before.

Fletcher and I both started in fright. We glanced at one another and then at Delapena, who was strangely unmoved on this occasion. He replaced his empty glass on the side table, his hand perfectly steady, and took a deep breath. "I believe it is my turn, gentlemen."

He smiled, rose, and walked to the door before either of us could protest.

We both stared after him and heard the door open. A few seconds later, I felt a draught of cold air. The clock ticked and the fire crackled, but there was no other noise. Ten seconds passed, then ten more. The room grew chill. Fletcher grasped the arms of his chair.

I stopped him: "I'll go."

Delapena's hat, stick, gloves, and cape were gone and the door was ajar. I opened it fully and looked out. It had stopped snowing. A single pair of footsteps led from our doorstep to the right. I could see two men walking down the hill; one was obviously Delapena, the other was very tall. As they passed beneath the street lamp, the tall man turned to Delapena. I could see his green spectacles in the gaslight. I closed the door and returned to the sanctuary of the sitting-room.

"Well?" asked Fletcher.

"I do not think we shall see Mr Delapena again," I replied.

Notes

The Last Testament: this story arose from my acquaintance with novelist David Tallerman during his residence in York. One of us (I can't remember which) suggested an exercise where we wrote one another's stories. This is the story I wrote from his plan; his story based on my plan is "The Hair of the Hound" (*Gaia: Shadow and Breath* 2, 2015). We also wrote our own stories: his is "Great Black Wave" (*Nightmare* 45, 2016); mine is "The Wolf Month", which makes its first appearance in this collection and takes a quote from "The Hair of the Hound" as its epigraph. The story of how the crawling chaos was averted, "The Lost Testament", will be the first of Roderick Langham's *Memoirs*.

The Colonel's Madness: given the social norms of the first hundred or so years of its existence, the award of the Victoria Cross has been remarkably egalitarian – crossing the barriers of class, nationality, and race – and just, with very few questionable awards. There were, however, some shenanigans surrounding several of the Anglo-Zulu War awards and I took the opportunity to combine my interests in military history and murder mystery in a single narrative. This adventure has also been published as "The Case of the Colonel's Suicide".

The Long Man: as with so many improbable tales, this one is based on historical fact. While Roderick Langham investigated his last case, the top thief-taker in the *Sûreté*, Inspector Robert Ledru, became the first recorded "homicidal somnambulist", across the channel in Le Havre. Ledru had to solve the murder himself – which, to his credit, he did – and his schizophrenia was caused by syphilis rather than toxoplasmosis.

The Tired Captain: like many of the forms of the genre, the armchair mystery has its origins in Poe, specifically his second Dupin story – "The Mystery of Marie Rogêt" (*Snowden's Ladies' Companion XVIII*, 1842-1843) – which suffers from being both too long and too restrained in its *dénouement*, the latter flaw courtesy of contemporary legal and/or social norms. All the information from *Dracula* (Constable, 1897) has been represented accurately and I suspect that the inconsistent arithmetic with regards to the crew of the *Demeter* was an error on Stoker's part rather than a device designed to cast doubt on the captain's state of mind.

The Wrong Doctor: there have been several controversies surrounding *The Hound of the Baskervilles* (George Newnes, 1902) and although the idea that Sherlock Holmes was wrong did not originate with me, I hope to have provided an original take on it. I explored the reasons for Doyle's oversight in an essay entitled "The Mystery of the Horrible Hound" (*Sherlock Holmes and Philosophy*, Open Court Books, 2011) and I explore the reason for Holmes' oversight here.

The Paradol Chamber: the identity of Allan Quatermain's son (or *sons*, which is part of the mystery) and Sebastian Moran's father are both disputed. We must not, of course, repeat Langham's mistake of attributing causation to coincidence, but I offered the first part of my solution in "Retirement home of the first action-hero" (*Dalesman 68*, 2006) and the second part here. The spatiotemporal coincidence of Holmes and the Ripper has been explored in numerous narratives of varied quality and length – Michael Dibdin's *The Last Sherlock Holmes Story* (Jonathan Cape, 1978) is by far the best. This adventure has also been published as "The Last Colonel Moran Story".

The Devil's Hollow: this was written for one of Robert M. Price's thus far unpublished projects, *The Derleth Mythos*, the theme of which is stories written in the style of August Derleth writing Lovecraft. I decided to imitate Derleth's mimicry by asking John Hall for permission to use his novelette, "Shaggai" (*Theaker's Quarterly Fiction 23*, 2008), as my backstory and to take the opportunity of Derleth's somewhat bizarre structuring of the Cthulhu mythos along elemental lines to allude to Gary Gygax and Frank Mentzer's *The Temple of Elemental Evil* (TSR, Inc, 1985), an Advanced Dungeons & Dragons campaign module that gave me a great deal of pleasure in my youth.

The Wolf Month: one of my two black dog stories, the other being "The Barghest" (Bards and Sages Publishing's *Society of Misfit Stories*, 2016). I am fascinated by the persistence of this legend, first through the incarnations of Black Shuck in East Anglia and the Barghest in Yorkshire, and second as revealed by the runaway success of *The Hound of the Baskervilles*. The epigram is a quote from Detective Fièvre, David Tallerman's occult detective, who has thus far appeared in two stories: 'Rindelstein's Monsters' (*The Death Panel: Murder, Mayhem, and Madness*, Comet Press, 2009) and "The Hair of the Hound".

The Christmas Cracker: this story was inspired by another acquaintance of mine, amateur historian Paul M. Chapman, who drew my attention to the link between Poe and Whitby in the person of Lowell. I used the idea to fulfil a long-time goal as a short fiction writer, to transform one of the plots M.R. James outlines in his "Stories I Have Tried to Write" into a short story, thus completing the work he began. I have sketched a speculative history of No.10 Flowergate in "Yorkshire's Greatest Detective" (*Around the Wolds & North Yorkshire 113*, 2007).

Printed in Great Britain
by Amazon